Inherited Courage

Also by Jane Bennett Gaddy

HOUSE NOT MADE WITH HANDS
THE MISSISSIPPI BOYS
ISAAC'S HOUSE
JOAB
RACHEL, AFTER THE DARKNESS
TO LOVE AGAIN

Inherited Courage

A Novel, After the War Years

For Glenda
with
Love.

Jane Bennett Gaddy

Jane Bennett Gaddy, Ph.D.

iUniverse®

INHERITED COURAGE
A NOVEL, AFTER THE WAR YEARS

iUniverse books may be ordered through booksellers or by contacting:

iUniverse
1663 Liberty Drive
Bloomington, IN 47403
www.iuniverse.com
1-800-Authors (1-800-288-4677)

ISBN: 978-1-5320-5780-9 (sc)
ISBN: 978-1-5320-5782-3 (hc)
ISBN: 978-1-5320-5781-6 (e)

Print information available on the last page.

iUniverse rev. date: 09/13/2018

Contents

PART TWO

Dedication

I owe a debt of gratitude to my Clark ancestors, sons and daughters of the Confederacy, those who fought on the *Southern Side of the Potomac*. And to the memory of Charlie Wayne Clark of Bruce, Mississippi, in Calhoun County, the keeper of all the Clark abiding memories, which he shared with me unreservedly.

He took me to Isaac's House in Slate Springs and told me the story. Charlie described Isaac as a *roguish* young southerner, and so he became my *rogue* character. I wrote *Isaac's House* knowing it, feeling it. Isaac Beauford Clark was but fifteen when the men went off to war. He ran away from home soon after in a futile effort to find his father and brothers, so he returned to the hills of Mississippi. When he was seventeen, he traveled hundreds of miles again, probably on horseback, to find his papa and brothers. His father sent him home just two weeks before our ancestors were killed on the Gettysburg Battlefield. At the appropriate time, he mustered in and stayed until the war ended. Isaac's house, in the woods at Slate Springs, Mississippi, is still the setting of an emotional story of the days after the war, when Carpetbaggers and Scalawags and Copperheads reared their menacing heads, and Reconstruction miserably failed at the hands of the Radicals, hence the given name of *Unreconstructed Southerners*. You need to know that phrase did not mean southern folks refused to become reconciled to some political, economic, or social change, but that the South could not be re-made in the image of the North or the Federal Government. It would never work, for the South believed and upheld States' Rights, a poignant story any way you view it.

Charlie painstakingly arranged a trip to the old Clark home place at Sarepta, on McGill Creek. I made my memories in those years. Unforgettable ones. Tears fill my eyes as I recall the time we spent with Charlie and Mary and members of our families. We roamed the old Clark home place, the hills, the valleys, McGill Creek with its walls of soapstone on one side and endless species of trees and brush on the other. And at the bottom, on the creek bed, lay the remaining rotting crossties that stabilized T.G. Clark's old gristmill, laid long before the war.

The day Charlie went to heaven was the day I lost a little bit of myself. Oh, I know I will see him again, for he is in the presence of Jesus. More than likely, amongst those he saw first were our dearly beloved Mississippi Boys—T.G., Jonathan, Albert Henry, Isaac, Joab and Samuel, and of course our great-great grandmother, Margery Brown Rogers Clark (Rachel in my books). Charlie lives on in our hearts, his knowledge of our ancestors remains the foundation on which we preserve our memories, and his love for those who trudged through tedious days and cold, dark nights of the Revolutionary War and the War for Southern Independence will give us strength and courage to forever bear the standard, I'm proud to share Charlie Clark's bloodline and love for the Old South. Truly—"Our General Has Gone Forward."

In Loving Memory of
Charlie Wayne Clark
December 31, 1928 – October 19, 2016
Bruce, Mississippi

"Let the tent be struck": victorious morning
Through every crevice flashes in a day
Magnificent beyond all earth's adorning:
The night is over; wherefore should he stay?
And wherefore should our voices choke to say,
"The General has gone forward?"

By Margaret Junkin Preston
Words uttered by Gen. Robert E. Lee as he lay dying,
Lexington, Virginia, October 12, 1870.

"Take the *Chauncey Vibbard* to Manhattan," Rachel had said.
"Every chance you get. And think of me."
Lee would always think of his grandmother.
She had been involved in every detail of his life,
always bringing back memories of his father and
grandfather who died at Gettysburg. And knowing her
as he did, she would be the inspiration behind any
success he hoped to glean from a future of
building skyscrapers and bridges.

But thou, O Lord, art a shield for me;
my glory, and the lifter up of mine head.

Psalm 3:3

Foreword

Jane Bennett Gaddy is a Southern Lady in the old and true sense of those words. She loves and remembers her ancestors, and she tells their stories as if she had known them face to face. Family, after all, is the most important part of life. She is a true daughter of the women who ran the farms and plantations and towns of the South while their men were dying shoeless in the snows of Northern Virginia. Soldiers have many fears during their service, and one of the worst, beyond death or maiming, is the fear that they will die in battle only to be forgotten. Even if they survive the War, will anyone ever care about what they suffered? Through Jane's books, our friends (her family) are not dead until they cease to be remembered, to which I always add, "May they never be forgotten." Jane has seen to it that her family lives on in the hearts of those who care.

I highly recommend *Inherited Courage* to those who wish to understand Southerners. You may well come to see family in a different light. You will be uplifted by the Christian character of the people portrayed. And you will see a bit of the results of the Great Revival in the Southern Armies during the Civil War. In shaking men to their very foundations, God brought many Southerners back to a true faith in Him and He deepened the faith of many more. Out of that terrible

War, God blessed the South, even to Southerners in this present decade. Jane and her writings are evidence of God's ongoing blessings.

I congratulate Jane that she is descended from such fine people. She has shown herself worthy of them by remembering and honoring their service to the South in the pages of her books.

Starke Miller
Oxford, University of Mississippi,
and Shiloh Historian
August 31, 2018

Starke Miller, former student at the University of Mississippi, twenty-eight years ago became interested in the University Greys, the Civil War Student Company that went to War from UM. Twenty-eight years he has chased them for a book, through libraries, archives, and across battlefields. Along the way he has stood in their houses, met their descendants, gone to school in the same buildings, and stood next to their graves. As one of two historians for the Eleventh Mississippi Memorial Committee, he has put markers at Gettysburg, Sharpsburg, and Gaines Mill. Starke moved to Oxford, Mississippi, to write factual books on the University Greys and all things Ole Miss connected to the Civil War. He also runs Civil War tours of Oxford/University and Shiloh.

Prologue

Her Chosen Altar—

Lee Payne sat alone aboard the driving seat of his step-grandfather's carriage at The Central Park stables. He pressed the old brown leather journal to his chest then let it drop to his lap, sucked in a deep breath of hot City air, and sighed as he pulled the strings to open it. The faithful horse snorted and moved about, conspicuously ready to trot Manhattan's cement streets.

"Okay, Dixie, I hear you." He closed the book and re-tied the strings without reading a word. No need. He knew what it said. He could repeat it without looking at the pages. He popped the reins and spoke aloud, "I, too, am ready, girl."

Somehow Lee thought Dixie understood every word he was saying. She responded with shoed hoofs pounding the cement streets, blinders firmly affixed, refusing to follow with her eyes, oblivious to the people, caring not that they rushed like the shallow waters under the bridges in The Central Park swirling through gutters and downspouts, splashing tediously beneath the grates of the City. They muttered caustically and then—ceased speaking, for Lee, like Dixie, had stopped hearing. Mercy and peace touched and became silent, like a fastidious cellar door that never bothered a soul.

No one had ever read the words from his journal that covered something over four years. Words he had written while dutifully and with pleasure satisfying his desire and allegiance to his country militarily and with as much dignity as he could muster, whilst at the same time fulfilling his lofty life-plan of preparing himself to design and build bridges and tall buildings.

No one had read the words he had written *beyond the black waters* of the Hudson River, beyond the thoughts of *the Come Line* and Sherman's heinous accomplishment of rape and pillage, killing and burning the Southland and its people, sewing the wind and reaping the whirlwind, for *it is appointed unto man once to die* ... including William T. Sherman.

Tucked inside was the letter Lee had written to his father who died in the heat of battle at Gettysburg. He would, one day, give it to his mother, Cassie Payne. No one had read it. Nor had anyone read carefully articulated entry of the hard earned education and the late night exchanges with those who thought they knew all about the South. No one knew that he had written about the sensitivities of the times, and about the many occasions, when persuaded by his personal integrity, he resisted the urge to hard-punch some ill-informed cadet who knew nothing about the South and its ideology, whose remarks were intended to insult and not exalt.

But, truth be known, those insulting times had been to his advantage. It would not have been worth it to fist fight his way through a conversation about the War for Southern Independence, not at West Point, though he was physically empowered. Occasions of this sort just heightened his structured scheme of fitness, and by the time he graduated, with honors, he was tough as shoe-leather.

He had worn the Gray, the swallowtail jacket, the plumes, and the sword in sheath strapped to his side. And he had followed the rules to the letter, making everyone he knew proud. For the rest of his life, he would be a member of The Long Gray Line. At the same time, he had prepared for a life in the City with the girl he loved, with one exception.

There had been no money left after he bought the ring at Tiffany's. He was working for his step-grandfather, Oscar Alexander, as a proofer and pressman at the lucrative newspaper, *The New York Elite Press*. But it was taking time to accumulate sufficient means to recover from purchasing the ring to marry Charlotte Jackson Elliott with enough remaining to rent an apartment and buy a small supply of food. His new job as a drafting and design engineer would not start until after the New Year.

With thoughts of how it had been and how it lingered—his financial dilemma—Lee wiped the perspiration from his face and slowed Dixie to a trot, followed the familiar route toward the Battery, and picked up speed until he reached the Harbor. He stopped the carriage at the rail and stepped down. How many times he had been to this peaceful haven. Alone. A herring gull screamed and flew over his head. Then ten more, each squawking and begging for food, a fish or mostly anything. It made no difference to them. He reached in his pocket and took out a handful of seeds he brought, knowing the pesky seabirds would keep coming back for more. But that was his point. He didn't want to be alone. He needed their temporary companionship, so he lured them. But in this moment, he wanted no human being around to invade his private thoughts. He tossed the seeds into the air, enticing the scavengers, watched as the broad-winged, barrel-chested gray-backs squawked and begged and harassed until they got more. And when they had scarfed all they could get, they snatched from the congregation, and when Lee had thrown out the last handful, they flew to the shoreline and perched on the mooring stakes, waiting for signs of better food options. From where he stood, he could see their pink legs and white heads, and for now that sufficed.

And so, Lee sat down on a park bench facing the Lady in the Harbor, remembering the blustery autumn day last year when President Grover Cleveland dedicated her. Lee had taken the boat ride to the Statue to be present at a sensational celebration. He thought of the tenement dwellers here in Lower Manhattan and the words of President Cleveland. *We will not forget that Liberty has here made her home; nor shall her chosen altar be neglected*. That was a lofty promise concerning her commitment and opportunity from her stationed perch at Bedloe's

Island, this gift from France symbolizing liberty and democracy and the alliance of the French and Americans during the Revolutionary War. It was all about the fight, wasn't it? Sometimes he wished he had been born in time to fight alongside his father, his grandfather, and his uncles, in the War Between the States. Was it every man's dream to be a fighter? To get the much-revered revenge, no matter how he did it?

It comforted him to know that the men of his family had been willing to fight, although it had not been necessary in their environment prior to the war. Certain things had spawned the whole idea—the responsibility for family and farm and freedom. And when all was said and done, the righteous desire to defend was stirred to every generation that followed and, knowing what he knew, and feeling the way he felt about his loved ones who fought, Lee had inherited a strong portion of that righteous desire, and for him, West Point had brought to maturity the mandate to protect, preserve, and defend.

He wiped his face again as the sweat dripped to his arms. It was hot, but his thoughts were equally scorching. Did he really want to taint the pages of this beautiful piece of leather with so disdainful a narrative as he became obsessed with certain intentions? Dare he characterize those intentions as such, and could not good come from evil? He thought of the Old Testament story of Joseph, how that his brothers, who cast him in the hole and left him for dead, had meant their wicked actions for evil, but God had meant them for good. If only he could think of his plans in that way.

Lee Payne leaned back on the park bench with his face toward the sun, his journal clutched to his chest as if it were some treasured manuscript ready for the publisher's consent. It was his; part of a life story. The good, the bad, and a vision of what the future might hold.

Part One

What a difference, what a contrast of cultures—
The lonesome strains of Dixie and the blaring,
raucous sounds of the Bowery Bands and street people.
How could a red-blooded American
choose one over the other?

Chapter

Stranger on the Street

Lee walked the sweltering streets of the Bowery. Raw garbage covered every available corner and spilled into and out of the alleyways. Sound, like the garbage, permeated the thick air, and the smell of rotting vegetables and dirt mixed with laughter from the street urchins and dogs barking filled his ears and eyes and nose as he tried in vain to justify his reasons for being here. He hadn't given himself access to this part of the city until now, and he was amazed at the cacophony of voices raised in every language. The world had landed on the Lower East Side of Manhattan, and he could feel his senses overload from the beauty of the experience and the pain of the poverty.

The streets, hard-packed with dirt a few years ago, were now white cement stained a grayish brown from traffic and the outdoor life of the poor. The summer months were unbearable indoors, and as Lee saw it, the less fortunate could move their entire lives outside to the city streets and courtyards and be far more comfortable.

From the fifth floor, an Italian immigrant, her ample frame filling the open window, a visual that what she offered would be worth the hours spent in the heat of an inadequate kitchen to prepare it, in heavy accent called out to her children on the street below, "Time for dinnah, Angelo! Get ya' brotha!"

The German girls in the tenement across the courtyard took to the fire escapes to reel in the laundry, hardly considered clean, flapping in the wind off the East River, a catch-all for the gray dust from the street. It was not without logic. Spin the rope on the pulley, take down the pins and the tattered clothing a piece at a time by drawing the rope monotonously and, in the process, celebrate yet another day of poverty.

The aroma of garlic and fresh tomatoes hand pressed through a cheesecloth sieve temporarily overpowered the stench of garbage, visions of a full stomach for some, and the streets began to empty for the dinner hour when body and soul were replenished for the time being. And afterwards, the young ones played and romped till midnight when they vied for the fire escape landings, the little waifs bent on being the first to call dibs on a cool place to sleep the night away.

Tomorrow would bring them to the streets again, barefoot boys with unbridled energy and a lust for life, where they would learn to be men or devils, depending on whether or not they had parents who cared.

Lee smiled as he thought of his own childhood under the hot Mississippi sun, wide-open spaces, hills and hollows, a deep cistern well into which he had dropped the oaken bucket a thousand times for cold, clear water. He suddenly longed for the musty fragrance and coolness of the shade of the sweet gum trees on McGill Creek, and he was aware once again of his shirt clinging tightly to his chest and the drag of his sweaty pant legs pulling against him as he walked the streets of the Lower East Side. He envisioned the pile of ragged overalls and hand-sewn flower-sack shirts on the hill above the cool waters of McGill and the adventure of scurrying down the soapstone to the bottom. Just Lee and his uncle Samuel who was only two years older than he.

The Bowery had evolved over the years, from once large and fertile farms owned and ruled by the Dutch, among whom was Peter Stuyvesant, born in 1592 in the Netherlands. He was the seventh and last of the Dutch director-generals, the same as governor, of New Amsterdam from 1647 to 1664. Stuyvesant was responsible for losing New Amsterdam and parts of New Netherlands to the British, after which he returned to the British West Indies for a time, then came back to the City renamed New York where he lived on his farm called *Bouerwie.* He died February of 1672 in the Bowery, his body entombed in the wall of St. Mark's Church. The City's history would always fascinate Lee. In his world, southerners buried their dead in the ground, not in the walls of churches. And just to remember the many names ascribed to this Granite Island was a true test of his knowledge of its history.

In the early 1800s, long before Lee was born, as the population of New York began to explode, the East Side became posh with fine stores and restaurants and theatres; and the people began to move to a quarter of the City that challenged Fifth Avenue in beauty. It was no longer fertile farm land, but a city in the making.

It was all about change, and change came to the Bowery again, so Lee was told, before the War Between the States started in April of 1861. That was when the once elaborate quarter gave way to German beer parlors and seedy flophouses, and the populace digressed to the most degenerate, yet the most colorful, of people. Now a lot of unscrupulous men lived in the neighborhood that had once housed fine respectable families.

Not unlike New York, Mississippi was once owned by other countries, the French and Spaniards in different quarters of the territory. But—in the War Between the States, and not in the same way as the ravages of Lower Manhattan and the immigrants' tenement district, crowded with people from every corner of the earth—much of the southern countryside had been burned and sacked, left desolate at the hands of the Union armies. Had the world as he had known it abandoned its moral compass and now become a sin-sick Sodom and Gomorrah? He thought so. It was that and much worse, now, especially in the lower quarters of Manhattan Island.

The City was amazingly colorful, full of history, but it lacked the dear folks, the southern hospitality, the deep abiding love and old familiar places—the get-aways for being alone and near to God.

He walked the street with a vision of what he was thinking of doing. But not really. How could he get a vision of *that*? The only reason he came here in the first place was because Grandmother Rachel had always told him about the days when she first arrived in the City, she would come to where the immigrants were stacked on top of each other like sardines, poor, wretched, and just slightly better off than the homeless. It was where the dregs of the earth could survive because they knew how to overcome hardness. As for Lee, his interest in this quarter of the City would only be for a few months, just until he could amass an amount of money sufficient to marry Charlotte and get a good start. He wanted quick money, but he wanted to work hard to earn it, he refused to do anything illegal, and he would maintain his integrity. That was the promise he made himself. He hardly knew where to start.

"Hey, mista, what you doing here?" Every bit of nine years old, the boy spoke authoritatively. Out of necessity, perhaps. Noticing someone new, a stranger on the street, sent up a warning signal. Lee allowed the boy had been taught as early as three years of age to help take care of the tenement folks.

"I was just watching you and your friends shoot marbles. What do you think I'm doing here?"

"Oh," he said, rolling the marbles in his hand. "Ya mean Knikkers? You don't look like you belong in here."

The boy spoke monotonously, mixing his answers with the same question, never looking up to make eye contact. How did he know Lee didn't belong there?

"You call it Knikkers?" said Lee.

"We're Dutch. We've always called it Knikkers."

Lee smiled and ruffled the boy's blond hair. "Well, I like it. I think that's what I'll call it to my friends and see if they know the difference."

"Yeah, that's a good idea."

He started to leave when the lad said, "Where're ya going?" with thoughts that he might be able to get the stranger to answer that question.

Lee was more interested in making friends with these street urchins than getting upset over the fact that the boy was nosey. After all, Lee was in his space. And, too, he had no reason not to take a liking to these young'uns who were less fortunate than most.

"I thought I would go for a cup of good Irish coffee if I find a place. Any ideas?"

"Over on East Seventh Street, Hannigan's Irish Pub. I here tell the coffee is good if you like whiskey."

"Thanks for the warning," said Lee, chuckling under his breath. "Amazing, a Dutchman like you knowing where the Irish Pub is located."

"We make it our business to know as much as possible," he said.

"Not a bad strategy," said Lee. "I'll see you next time."

"Hope so. So long for now."

Chapter 2

The Weight of Sadness—

The boy never looked up. Lee, allowing he had eyes in the back of his head, turned to go with intent of finding the Irish pub, when a young man who looked to be thirteen, though quite undernourished, rendering it impossible to determine his precise age, rounded the corner on a fairly fine looking bicycle but without the wherewithal to stop, obviously in the absence of sufficient brakes. Barely missing Lee, he shouted out an apology.

"I'm sorry, sir!"

"That bicycle of yours is a handful, I believe. But, my, it's a nice one."

It was all the boy could do to manage the Boneshaker, a painful ride with a wrought-iron frame and wooden wheels overlaid with iron.

"Yes sir," he said, trying hopelessly to bring the monster into subjection. "It pretty much eats into the flesh sometimes. Everything about it is cruel."

He had a crop of curly auburn hair, a strong accent, shabby and definitely not scrubbed. The Boneshaker sort of aligned with his apparent lifestyle. Rough as a corncob, but well spoken. And … maybe life had been cruel.

"Where'd you get that?"

"Mr. Hannigan gave it to me. 'Twas in the alley back of the pub and when nobody claimed it—well, it became mine."

"Hannigan, huh?"

"Yes sir. I work there when he needs me."

Lee sat down on the dirty curb and motioned for the boy to sit beside him. For some reason, he was compelled to know this young man's story. Without hesitating, the lad sat down next to Lee.

"How old are you, son?"

"Almost thirteen, I think."

"Don't you know?"

"Not exactly." And in the sharp but beautiful Irish accent, the boy began to speak. "I have no birth papers. M' story is a little complicated, sir."

"I would like to hear it."

With nothing to lose, the street urchin began to weave an affecting story.

"M' grandmother and grandfather wer' born in Ireland. M' grandfather fell sick during the potato famine, tried to work his land and save his crops whilst so many wer' leaving Ireland and coming here to United States. M' father was young, just seven years old. He tried to help, but m' grandfather died from some illness, m' thinks having to do with the famine. Not long after, m' grandmother died, leaving m' father alone to fare for himself. M' father was an orphan.

"When he was about twenty-three years old, he came to America, but at the awf'list time. Have y' heard of the Draft Riots?"

"Yes. Yes, I have, son. It was during the American Civil War, or as we call it in the South, the War for Southern Independence, as it was not really a Civil War. What happened to your father? Don't tell me he fought in the streets of the City."

"That he did. From what I've found out since, it was the worst thing that ever happened here. In a small way, as bad for the streets of New York as the Civil War was for the South. The black Africans and the Irish immigrants fought over jobs and they fought the system for the draft imposed by y'r President Lincoln. Hardly anyone had money to pay the politicians to get them off the hook for the draft. It cost something like three hundred dollars. M' father never saw that much money in his life, I'm sure. He was not a citizen anyway, so I don't suppose it mattered as far as he was concerned. When the draft hit, men who had money could buy their way out of serving in Mr. Lincoln's army, but the City's poor working men didn't have the money, so they had to go to war.

"Well, what started out as an opposition turned into a violent uprising that involved the wealthy, the Black Africans, the Irish, and that Civil War itself. For four days, they fought in the streets. A few blacks wer' hanged down here, probably by the Irish Catholic men. New York City was in trouble.

"My papa had left his sweetheart in Ireland hoping to bring her to America. Things wer' so bad here that his hopes failed and he returned to Ireland several years after the war when he had saved enough money for passage. That's when he married m' mother. A year later, I was born, and after two years, m' mother and father sailed, once again, for America. M' father took sick on the ship and just a few days before we arrived in America, he died. He was buried at sea and so wer' a lot of other Irish immigrants who didn't make it. M' mother kept a small picture of them by her bed—always, so I could grow up knowing what m' father looked like."

Lee closed his eyes and fought his emotions. He swallowed hard and listened quietly.

"It was awful for m' mother, and me, too, I suppose. I don't remember anything about when we first arrived here. M' mother always told me about m' father, though."

"Where's your mother?"

And as if the conversation had not become heart-breaking enough, without hesitating, the boy explained with little emotion, whether false or conjured, "She died about six months ago. Took pneumonia right at Christmastime—and died. That left me with no one, but I was big enough to take care of m'self, something like eleven or twelve years old. I'm an orphan, but m' father made it for awhile. Maybe I can, too."

Lee dropped his head and gasped. It was all he could do to keep from crying out. This lad had suffered inconceivable loss, yet he held his head up and conversed with Lee like a man.

"What's your name, son?"

He stretched out his hand, politely reaching for Lee's. "M' name's Malachi O'Malley."

Lee gladly took the dirty hand. "That's a fine name. How do you spell that?"

"M-a-l-a-c-h-i. You know like in the Bible, only you pronounce it Mala-*kee* not *i*. I'm Irish, not Jewish."

"My name's Lee. Robert E. Lee Payne. You can call me Lee."

"I've heard of Robert E. Lee. He's the famous southern general, I think."

"You're absolutely right," said Lee, wondering how he knew. "My father died, too, fighting in General Lee's Army of Northern Virginia in the War Between the States when I was only a year old. He never got to see me and, of course, like you, I never knew my father."

"Splendid! Seems like that would be a better way to die than just getting sick."

"I've never thought of it that way. I'll have to ponder that. And so where do you live, Malachi?"

"To be perfectly honest with y', Mr. Lee, I live on the street." Though a bit embarrassed, Malachi respectfully relinquished his personal information, after which he sighed deeply and dropped his thin shoulders. Truth be known, he felt better that someone knew something about him.

Lee clinched his teeth and did not reply. He was incensed that a City this big and this full of wealth could not do something about young children, orphaned, and living on the streets.

"Did you say you work some at Hannigan's?"

"Yes sir."

"How would you like to go there with me? I don't rightly know the way, and it would be helpful if you would show me. We can put your Boneshaker on the back of my carriage."

"That would be splendid." Malachi, smiling broadly, was not the least bit reluctant.

They rode through the East Side to Cooper Square past a few posh buildings and beautiful churches with Malachi leading the way, happy to have a smart adult with whom to chat.

"Do you know where a bicycle repair shop is around here, Malachi?"

"Y' just passed one a block east. It's behind another building, but I know how to get there. And begging y' pardon, Mr. Lee, 'tis pronounced Malach-ee."

Lee smiled, turned around at the next street, tapped his horse for a little speed, and followed Malachi's direction. They passed Cooper Union, an educational institution that Peter Cooper founded in 1859. Lee was familiar with the history of the college and its founder. It was where men and women learned any and everything having to do with architecture and engineering and art. *The art of building skyscrapers, he mused.* Cooper, of Dutch descent, was born in New York City, his father a lieutenant in General George Washington's Army. Peter Cooper was a prominent New Yorker, known for having done a little of everything. He even ran for President of the United States, invented some things, and put together *The Tom Thumb* from musket barrels and some scraps of small steam engines. John Quincy Adams signed his patent. And—he had definitely been on the other side of the War Between the States, closely associated with The Radical Reverend Mr. Henry Ward Beecher—

"There," Malachi yelled, pointing toward an old shop building, scarcely visible from the street, but he knew it was there. "Stop at the rail."

It was, indeed, a bicycle repair shop with scanty fixtures and a hard-packed dirt floor. From the looks of it, the proprietor, also a seller of certain other bicycle and carriage parts and supplies, had not yet taken the opportunity to make it fancy like the other places of business around him. But—Lee marveled that this triangle of progress on the East Side was all about excessively stretching brain and brawn to full capacity. No doubt this old shop and its owner had been here on this spot for ages and the City was building itself around them.

"Now, let's take this monster down and see if we can get something done."

"But Mr. Lee, I don't have money for bicycle repairs. Actually, I don't have money—a'tall."

"Well, let's just say that this will be a gift if it works."

The boy's eyes lit up. To have a real ride would be amazing. Lee could scarcely keep from getting emotional again. Homeless and no way to get around. Confinement to a few blocks in a city of this magnitude was—it was unacceptable.

The repairman hovered over the frame of a carriage with parts spread out on all sides.

"I beg your pardon, sir, is there any way you can take these wood wheels and iron covers off and put some rubber wheels on this boy's Boneshaker?"

He wiped the grease off his hands and took a cursory look through spectacles that were dripping with sweat, pulled out a less than clean rag from his pocket and wiped them off so he could see.

"Then 'twouldn't be a Boneshaker a'tall," he said, laughing at himself. "I can tell you right now, it's not possible, sir. There's nothing to mount the tires on. But would the boy be willing to trade that bicycle for a good one with usable rubber tires? This Boneshaker can be fixed, but it will take some money to get it into good shape. I can sell it like it is with little effort."

Lee's heart jumped to his throat. But what about Malachi? The boy was grinning from ear to ear as the repairman brought out a nice bicycle with rubber wheels.

"I went over this one with a fine-toothed comb, and painted it m'self. I always think a boy's bicycle should be red, so that's the color I chose."

Malachi's smile doubled its size, revealing a row of perfectly shaped pearly white teeth and immense satisfaction.

"Do you think Mr. Hannigan would mind if you traded the Boneshaker, Malachi?"

"Oh, no sir! The bicycle didn't belong to him, anyway, and he won't care. He was only trying to discard it when he offered it to me. Some kid dumped it on the alley behind his place just to get rid of it. He'll be proud to know what I got in exchange for it."

"Then if it's a deal, here's your bicycle and two dollars besides, and I'll take the Boneshaker, son. It's a good trade for both of us, I don't mind telling you."

"Well, this is the best day of m' life," said Malachi, clutching the dollar bills like they were gold. He stuffed them into the corner of a ragged pocket, they thanked the repairman profusely, and rolled the new ride to Lee's carriage then boarded.

"I am most appreciative of the nice bicycle, Mr. Lee, and afraid I'm caught without words."

"Now, where are you going to keep it, son. That is, since you don't have a place to live."

"All I can tell y' is that it will stay right with me."

"Let's go to Hannigan's. Which way, Malachi?"

"Back to Cooper Square, which used to be Stuyvesant Square. You know, for Peter Stuyvesant, the Dutchman who was rich and lived around here and died in the Bowery?"

"You know a lot, Malachi, especially about this part of Manhattan."

"I know Manhattan used to be called New Amsterdam. A lot of Dutch stuff. Not much Irish of significance."

"Will you be allowed to sit with me at the bar? I want you to introduce me to Mr. Hannigan."

"Yes, sir!"

Lee pushed the swinging doors open, scarcely able to take everything in at one time. *A real saloon, he thought. Looks like the Wild, Wild West.* The place was authentic with a pot-belly stove for the winter months, sawdust on the floor, likely for the excess of whatever may get puked up or spilt during the course of an afternoon and evening. Lee had never seen communal tobacco pipes, but there they were. Brass spittoons he recognized, thinking about the old men who dipped and spit in the square at Sarepta. Ensconced in front of the wall of mugs of myriad sizes and shapes, was a wooden bar with stools, and wooden tables and chairs were scattered on the open floor. The lower walls were covered with old pictures and memorabilia. Framed and hanging behind the bar was an original 'Wanted' sign for John Wilkes Booth, the man who shot President Lincoln. It would likely stay forever. Lee decided he had best not let it be known he was the real son of a Confederate soldier killed in battle. After all these years, the war could still be a touchy subject for many. And, too, this was the typical smelly, noisy, crowded saloon where only stout-hearted and muscled males were allowed in.

Lee was a coffee drinker. Had been all his life. His grandmother served him spoons of honey-sweetened heavy cream in a half cup of coffee from the time he was a year old to the present. He had been in New York long enough to know that the best coffee in the City was in the Irish pubs. Now if he could have it his way, everything would be fine. That remained to be seen.

Mr. Hannigan served ale two ways, light or dark and that's all. No in between. Mattered not to Lee, for he would never drink the stuff. But somehow he knew the coffee would be splendid. He and Malachi climbed onto bar stools, Lee allowing it was too late in the boy's life to worry about the appearance of evil.

"What would you like, son?"

"What I call a milk coffee, please. Mr. Cavanaugh knows what I like. He's here tonight, and I don't think Mr. Hannigan is here."

Cavanaugh took orders and drew ale for his other customers, gave a little wave to Malachi and soon approached Lee.

"What'll it be, sir?"

"A milk coffee, Malachi style, please. And I'll have an Irish coffee, hold the whiskey if you're going to burn it off. Frothy milk or cream, and a little nutmeg grate on the top."

"Yes sir," said the bartender. "Obviously you don't drink? Don't let Mr. Hannigan know that. He might have you removed."

"I hope not," said Lee. "It's hard to get a better coffee than from the Irish. But that's my way of life. No alcohol for me, not now, not ever, so if that's a problem ..."

"No sir," he said. "It's not a problem for me, and Mr. Hannigan is off tonight."

He threw his head back and laughed heartily. Lee and Malachi joined him. When he left to fill the order, Malachi said, "You really want to do this, Mr. Lee?"

"Do what, Malachi?"

"Drink coffee instead of ale? You know to be Irish and not drink is a sin, and the Irish will rule the world."

"You don't really believe that, do you, Malachi? For how can anyone rule the world when they don't know their head from a hole in the ground?"

Malachi looked up at Lee and they both broke into loud guffaws, sufficient to make up for all the lack of ale-drinking. The Irish would have to settle for some lilting laughter instead of a drunken stupor.

Malachi ran his hand across the polished wood rail that held him safely onto the leather seat. "Nice rig y' got, Mr. Lee."

"It belongs to my step-grandfather, Mr. Oscar Alexander, and yes, it's very nice, thank you. This horse, Dixie, has endeared herself to me. I'm beginning to think of her as my own."

Oscar Alexander was from British royalty, and he had made a fine life in Manhattan for many years. His first wife died giving birth to Oscar's only child, a son. The boy died the same day, leaving Oscar grief-stricken and lonely.

"My grandmother, Rachel Payne, from a little hill town in Mississippi called Sarepta, had hoped to become a journalist after the war. She answered an ad in *The New York Elite Press,* a newspaper owned by Mr. Alexander. Rachel's mother had sent her all of the New York papers during and after the war, and long story short, Mr. Alexander hired her, never having seen her, based on some articles she sent in answer to his ad for a featured journalist."

Lee continued the short story about his grandmother, hoping he was not boring Malachi. He really didn't know why he was so drawn to the young street urchin, but for some reason, he wanted Malachi to know at least as much about him as Malachi had told him about his own tragic life.

"Rachel was, and is, an encourager for the women of the South whose husbands died in battle. Later, during Reconstruction and the aftermath of war, she reached out to both northern and southern women as time passed. No doubt she helped thousands of young widows who read her articles in *The Elite Press.*

"My grandmother has a magnificent story concerning the South, Malachi. And when I determined to go to West Point Military Academy, she was right here for me. She and Mr. Oscar live on the Upper East Side and while they're away, I take care of their home and carriage and Dixie. They go to Sarepta in Mississippi for half of the year, so my grandmother can be in her old familiar place as much as possible. You see, her husband, my grandfather, Thomas Goode Payne, died at Gettysburg. My stepfather is my Uncle Jonathan, who married my mother a year or so after my father died in that same battle. So … the short story ending, my grandfather and his two sons fought in Gen. Lee's Army of Northern Virginia, and then when my Uncle Isaac was old enough, he joined the Mississippi Cavalry and fought till the war ended."

"That is an amazing story, one of which I would love to learn more," said Malachi.

Lee pulled the carriage into the neighborhood where he had found his new friend and said, "Well, Malachi—spelled with an *i,* but pronounced with two *e's*—I hope I see you again someday so we can continue the story."

Tears welled in the young man's eyes as he jumped to the ground and retrieved his new bicycle with rubber wheels.

"We will meet again, Mr. Lee." He choked, mounted his bicycle, and smoothly rode off without looking back.

Meeting Malachi the way he did was past Lee's understanding. He related to the boy, yet he couldn't come up with a good reason as to why this had all taken place. He believed that every event in life had a purpose. Moreover, he believed that for every experience, God had His own private plan and that sometimes He revealed those plans. It was significant that the boy was raising himself with no parents, no papers, and in a foreign country. His words echoed in Lee's ears. *We will meet again, Mr. Lee.*

He would head back to the Upper East Side soon, but before he did, Lee tapped Dixie, pointing her toward the Battery. He pulled to the otherwise empty curbside, and sitting on the carriage, and looking out into the murky water, he watched the waves beat against the sea wall. Through the mist, he could see her there in the port of entry and thought of the poem inscribed upon the monument of the Lady. *Give me your tired, your poor, your huddled masses yearning to breathe free; the wretched refuse of your teeming shores, send these the homeless, tempest-tossed to me. I lift my lamp beside the golden door.*

"The Golden Door," he said aloud. "The Golden Door? *This* is the Golden Door?" And to himself, he said, *Malachi lives in the Gilded City, the city of hope and desire. On the filthy streets of the Bowery on the Lower East Side of the richest city in the world.*

Lee could not breathe deeply enough of the salty sea air to rid himself of the foul-smelling tenement dwellings. He could not cry enough tears to cleanse himself of the sights and sounds of poverty. He could not stifle his thoughts of Malachi working in a saloon for a few pennies to buy bread just to stay alive, to live one more day in search of a fire escape on which to sleep, on which to block out the memory that he had no father, no mother—no one upon whose shoulder to lean.

He got out and sat on the park bench overlooking the harbor, fixating on the Custom House where all these people flocked in, year after year, filling up the tenement dwellings, filling up the streets. *What kind of wretched countries had they come from, he wondered? Is this country so much more saintly that it could take care of the yearning masses?*

There must be a lesson here, thought Lee. He dropped his rig at the Central Park livery, walked across the street, and bent under the weight of sadness, took the steps to the third floor of the stylish Brownstone apartment and fell across the bed on which his grandmother Rachel always kept clean linens and fine pillows. He was man enough to cry himself to sleep, wondering where on earth Malachi slept in the winter months. And how did he stay warm?

Lee awoke the next morning with swollen face, thinking he had been dreaming. As usual, he ran down the three flights to the porch, retrieved two quart bottles of milk left by the wagon, and looked out over The Central Park across the street. This was tree-covered heaven. Surely it wasn't an extension of the same city where Malachi barely eked out an existence.

He drank his coffee, wishing he were sitting on the barstools with Malachi, watching over him, making sure he had a hot cup of milk coffee and a place to stay just one more night. He thought of the red-painted bicycle with rubber wheels and managed to smile.

Feeling immensely blessed to have temporary access to an inside bathing room with running water and clean, white towels, Lee looked into the mirror and found his image to be quite handsome, but mostly satisfied the cool cloths had fixed his swollen eyes. He brushed his dark damp hair and combed it into his favorite style, donned the freshly starched and ironed white blouse, slipped the garters over the sleeves, and took a carriage taxi to *The Elite Press*, looking like a newspaper proofer.

"Good morning, Carlisle."

Carlisle Peterson had worked for Oscar Alexander for years, from the time he was fifteen. Oscar had rescued him from much the same situation as Malachi. Now, many years later, Carlisle ran the newspaper for Mr. Alexander. Lee doubted life got more successful than that.

"Good morning, Lee."

"How was the night, Carlisle? Any breaking news?"

"No. Everything seems to be in good order, and I'll be going now that you're here. There's a telegram from Mr. Alexander and your grandmother. Nothing new in Sarepta. They're just checking to make sure all is well in the City and with you and me."

Lee wished he could say all was well with him. Maybe it was good that he needed money badly enough to consider what he was about to consider, else he would never have run into the poor wretch, Malachi. He must see him again, that is, if he could find the needle in a haystack. He looked up at Carlisle, who was preparing to leave for the day, as it was his duty to work all night. *I want a Carlisle in my life, he thought. A brother he has become in these years. I want another brother like Carlisle Peterson.*

He would go to Hannigan's again in a few days. He needed to get on with his plan before he changed his mind. He didn't even know where to start.

The press room was alive and running as he began proofing. This was a splendid job and he loved working at the newspaper. But he was trained to touch the landscape, to make a difference, and one day to build a skyscraper and touch the sky. But first he was focused on earning enough money to start a life with Charlotte. He loved her beyond words, and he knew she loved him and that she would wait, but he was reluctant to believe she would *want* to wait too much longer. It was over four years ago that they had pledged to marry. Neither had money to travel often and he missed her. Oh, how he missed her.

The presses rumbled and the tele-communicators clicked off messages with noises sufficient for Lee to do his job while blocking out the thoughts of what could be happening to his young friend, Malachi.

Chapter 3

A Remarkable Story

"What's wrong with y', Payne? Are y' dying? Y' come in here and order coffee when y' could be having a nice light or dark ale? And y' don't even have a hangover?"

Lee was meeting the man for the first time, and he was surprised but glad that Mr. Hannigan knew who he was. He took his chances on getting tossed out when he explained his stand against strong drink of any sort—and that in Mr. Hannigan's own Irish Pub.

"This is how it is, Mr. Hannigan. I'm a Christian, and I know it's wrong to drink because I know what it does to a man. I've seen it in every walk of life. If you let the habit attach itself to you and you don't have the stamina, or maybe grace, to stop when you've had enough—well, you know that story, Mr. Hannigan. It's not something I want to do to myself. Also, it's tradition in my family. We don't touch the stuff. That gives us one less worry in life. So … you'll never see my puke mixed with the sawdust on your floors. But, I do love your coffee, sir."

"Y're killin' me, Payne!"

After that elucidation, Lee had no idea that Mr. Hannigan would let him stay, but it was best to get it out in the open. It was his conviction and he would stick to it or he would not be able to come back to Hannigan's anyway. There was method in madness for coming here in the first place, and he would leave it at that.

Hannigan ranted briefly, re-charging a rogue Irish demeanor then continued a more peaceful conversation with Lee.

"Okay, I promise not to throw y' out. Besides, I hear tell y've taken a liking to Malachi. At least, I know he's taken a liking to you, and that makes m' happy. I wish I could do more for the boy, but I don't have a place for him to stay, and he refuses to go to an orphanage. I can't blame him for that. He says it would be a step below the disaster he came from. In Ireland, that is. His mother, before she died, told him how deplorable it was and that he must always be glad he came to America. In the long run, it would prove to be the best life for him. He seems to make it okay. I think the scamps out there know which fire escape he likes to sleep on. He's not a fighter, but he could be one if the occasion arises. He talks a good game. Don't know where he gets it, but I hear him using street talk for the fight, if you know what I mean."

"You're right about me taking a liking to him. He's a fine boy to have been brought up by the hair of the head. I think the street talk is his means of defense, a way of protecting himself because he's alone. And, no I don't know what you mean about *the fight*." Lee answered Hannigan with little inquisitiveness. He would address that later.

"You from the South?"

"Yes sir. Should I try and disguise my accent and my colloquialisms a little better? I see you still have the 'Wanted' poster for John Wilkes Booth."

"No, son! The war's over. That's just a reminder of how it was."

"Sometimes I wonder if the war is really over, sir."

Lee spoke in a quieter voice as he often did when remembrances of the war came into the conversation.

"When you lose part of your family to the fight, you think it will never be over. The South barely survived Lincoln's death blow. I grew up in Mississippi, not too far from Oxford, home of the University.

Union Forces burned most of the town to the ground, including the beautiful old Courthouse. You may not know this, but the University of Mississippi gave up much blood and treasure to the muster. Fifty of the two hundred and twenty-eight students of the 1860-1861 class joined the University Greys, along with a hundred men who were not students. Thirty-three of that number made it to Gettysburg. One was mortally wounded in the cannonade that preceded Pickett's Charge and thirty-one went into the charge. Fourteen were killed and seventeen were wounded that day. That's a hundred percent casualties.

Hannigan listened intently, polishing the same place on the bar over and over until he realized what he was doing.

"That's a very interesting story you tell," he said quietly. "How do you know that to be true, son?"

"My father, Albert Henry, his brother, Jonathan, and their father, who, of course, was my grandfather, fought on the first day of that battle. It was July 1, 1863. My father and grandfather were killed on that day. Jonathan is now my stepfather. Sometime before that battle, my father left Jonathan a letter in the bottom of his haversack, requesting that he marry my mother and take care of me if he; that is, my father, were killed in battle. I know that's confusing to everyone but me. On July 2, Jonathan buried my father and grandfather in the same shallow grave on the battlefield. That's how I know the story about the University Greys is true. Oxford, Mississippi, and the University were well represented in that battle. The next day, July 3, they fought on the same hill as my stepfather, Jonathan, at Pickett's Charge. So you might say I heard it from the horse's mouth, not the grapevine.

"I know just about everything about the fight in the Eastern Theatre of the war. Jonathan, my father now, has told me. It was of great importance to me and my class at West Point. I've made it my business to study each of the amazing Confederate generals who fought for the South. And, too, I'm engaged to a beautiful southern girl from Lexington, Virginia, home of Stonewall Jackson for at least ten years before he was killed. My family fought with Lee. Hers fought with Jackson. Her father was killed at Chancellorsville. So was General Jackson, of course."

Hannigan took in a deep breath and turned his back to wipe a tear.

"I've been entrenched at this bar for so many years, I guess I didn't get a lot of the story, even while it was happening." He reached to take the 'Wanted' poster off the wall.

"Sir! Please don't. I didn't tell my story for that purpose. I'm a New Yorker now, at least fifty percent. I graduated from West Point Military Academy, up the Hudson, and I've met men from all walks of life, from every state of the Union, and we all have a story to tell about our fathers who fought. But we *are* a Union now. Lincoln had a mind of his own, and we each are deserving of our opinion about him. I'll just say I'm glad it was not a southerner who showed up in Ford's Theatre on that particular evening. At least, I don't recall that Maryland ever seceded from the Union."

"I see what y' mean. Thank y' for sharing y'r story, son. 'Tis a remarkable one. And on that last thought, I'll just have to say, I'm glad to be of Irish descent. We had our own war on the streets of New York during that time, if y' recall, and sometimes we wonder if it will ever end."

"Thank you for listening, sir. It's been a pleasure meeting you. And, yes, my grandmother told me all about the Africans and the Irish fighting it out in the streets of New York during the war years. Obviously, there were not enough jobs to go around. The grounds are different, but the principle is the same. The South was fighting for homes and farms and families. *The tired, the poor, the huddled yearning masses* were fighting for scraps of food and a table to put them on."

"Y're right about that, Payne. Will y' come again? I'd like to talk about that violent disturbance in Lower Manhattan. I'll never forget it. Actually, it happened exactly twenty years ago this week—July 13-16, 1863. They called it Draft Week. Y' should have been sitting right there twenty years ago, Payne." Hannigan pointed to where Lee was sitting, bringing it closer to home. "The Irishmen spewed out more hate for the United States President Lincoln than you can imagine. Three full days I listened as they filled my ears with their complaints. These men had fought every battle imaginable just to get out of Ireland and onto the shores of this Country only to continue the fight for jobs and food when they got here. It was a mess. The streets were moving live with working-class men, resenting the wealthy, resenting Lincoln for the way he shaped and formed the draft, resenting those who expected something for nothing when they had to scrap for a morsel of food. If you had three hundred dollars, a large sum of money, money the Irish-poor didn't have, you could avoid the draft. There was a lot of cursing going on here for those three days.

"Sorry Payne, I didn't mean to rant. And I say, will y' come back?"

"You bet, as long as you will prepare me that splendid Irish coffee. I do like the ale burnt, though it may seem like cheating. It keeps me from breaking a promise to myself and gives me that splendid Irish flavor at the same time. We will talk more about the war days when I come back. Good day, sir."

Lee had been grazing a little close to the edge, spiritually speaking. But from his perspective the greater good was at stake. He knew what he was doing, and his purpose was as pure as the driven snow, though his grandmother would call it—the burnt ale—*the appearance of evil.* He combed the Lower East Side and the Bowery, looking for a bicycle and an auburn-haired Irish boy. The sun was dropping on the Hudson River side, and after dark it would be impossible to see him amongst the innumerable Dutch, Irish, and German boys, each speaking their own language or attempting to speak a friend's language, many of them less than fluent in at least three.

Lee would try another day. He switched his horse and turned the carriage down an unfamiliar street. The sun disappeared below the buildings and darkness settled over the East End. Seedy side streets and alleys emptied up their drunken men and they stepped out into the path of traffic. Lee realized it was not someplace he needed to be at this time of day. He felt sorry for these drunken immigrants who had never truly experienced the *American Dream* but had lived more of the extended nightmare that followed them across the Atlantic Ocean, leaving behind a country that had obviously failed and forgotten them.

He hoped they could, at some sweet time, break out of poverty and find the beauty of a free country, one that he had experienced every day of his life as he remembered it.

He drove, only partially aware of where he was. The street noise was growing louder with sounds unfamiliar to him, so loud that he had an inclination to stop. He would stay in the carriage, not wanting to lose it to thieves. He wasn't too sure of himself.

He waited until someone came near who was not staggering or slurring his words. The reality that there were no women anywhere around told him a lot. *A man's world down here, he thought. Not a safe place for a decent woman. Not a safe place for anyone!*

"Excuse me, sir," Lee shouted. "Why all the noise and disturbance?"

"Oh, this is but mild. The fight's just getting started."

"The fight? I don't see a fight," said Lee. "The noise seems to be coming from that building on the corner."

"Yeah, that's it," said the stranger. "The fight's in there. Ever heard of boxing?"

"Yes." Lee felt hot water fill his mouth, his adrenaline at the boiling point. "Are you speaking of bare-knuckle fighting?"

"Yeah, bare-knuckle. Tonight's the big one, the stakes pretty high."

Lee was terrified. This was the place he had wanted to *find*. What street was he on? And why was he shaking from head to toe? At the moment he didn't even know his own name, and he didn't like the feeling at all. Was it conviction? At the same time, gravity was pulling him toward that building and the piercing noise. He dared to step down and tie his horse and carriage to the post, realizing the reason these men were here was not to steal his rig but for the momentary thrill of the bloody fight. If he didn't do it now, he may never. Inching closer, straining to see over the heads of tall, raucous men, he breathed in something he had never smelled before. Strange, putrefying body fluids of a thousand different nationalities. Lee choked. He wasn't sure how much his system could tolerate. Dirty men, some with beards, some not, most skinny, all underfed, unclean and overheated, sweating in the hot July evening. A couple of slow whirling two-blade ceiling fans moved the stench about. Without it, they would have stifled.

Lee's plan had been churning inside him for weeks and this was his terminus, a full-orbed revelation. He had found the place. He couldn't help it; he was compelled to draw in a deep breath then felt sick. Now the stench was in his nostrils to stay. Had he lost his mind? The only person in his family that would dare to do something like this was his once roguish Uncle Isaac. This place had all the trappings of evil. In pondering the whole of the environment, he wondered what made him think he could do this in the first place. It wasn't the lust for the fight. It wasn't even the lust for money. It was a longing to make something happen quickly and as painlessly as possible. At this moment, hearing the groans and less than sympathetic shouts from the crowded room as the fighters took the blows whilst their blood sprayed across the dirty mat, he wondered if his plan could be carried out—*painlessly.*

The foul odor was near unbearable, and the cigar smoke boiled out into the street, making Mr. Hannigan's place look like a ladies' afternoon tea. He couldn't see much at all. Lee had heard about the toxic filthiness of tobacco curing and cigar rolling in the tenements of German immigrants. It was their way of making a living. A pittance of pay and everyone who breathed or puffed suffered. Now Lee was included in this number.

He backed out into the street listening to the shouts of men and boys, those who were old enough to enter without getting in trouble. And then he heard the screeching yelps—not a manly growl or shout or otherwise reaction to a blow to a body part, but the sound of a dog being attacked. He turned to one of the men standing near his rig and asked the question, "What on earth is that?"

"Oh, a bitah be in dat ring."

Suddenly Lee was glad he could not see what was unfolding on the other side of the sea of disheveled heads and flailing arms raised in a tent-like cover of protection over the ringside.

"What?" Lee was indignant, but he was too far into this conversation to back out, besides he had already risked his life to come here—to find out—

"Yeah, a bitah, and dat po' boy got no idea how to deal wif' it. He de one making de blood-curdling noise, but he can't help it. I hear tell it hurts worse than anything you can imagine. It's not a legal move, but dat fighter, he always get by wif it."

The man, black as the night sky, was haughty, proud to know more than Lee. He was an immigrant with an Island accent and the clothes on his back were rotten from years of wear. Lee didn't care. He would never have judged him based upon what he had or did not have. He just filed the information into his brain cell and quickly boarded.

"Which way out of the Bowery, sir?" he asked the man.

"Where you go mah'n?"

"Fifth Avenue. I'm turned around," said Lee reluctantly. The man looked at him like he didn't have good sense. Lee realized his southern vernacular had taken over.

"I came down to Hannigan's and lost my direction," he explained, trying not to sound too disgusted or too southern.

"Den go right up heah to Canal Street, take a lef' to Broadway, turn right. Dat's de best and easiest way to get outa heah. You should see somethin' familiar up Broadway. It's dahk, so just watch for de street signs."

"That should get it for me. I'm familiar with Broadway at Canal. Thank you, sir."

"You be ca'ful now, southern boy."

The man had no idea that what he said didn't offend Lee Payne at all, though he meant it to be offensive. Lee was just thankful for the directions from a sober man. He made no eye contact as he left. Grandmother Rachel would die if she knew he were down in the Bowery at dark.

Chapter

For Malachi's Sake—

It was like a recurring nightmare, and as hard as Lee tried, he could not release himself of the hideous memory; he could not separate himself from the screams of the poor man in the boxing ring the night he dared venture deep into the Bowery. While all that was true, he had to admit everything had unexpectedly fallen into place that night. Now he must figure out a means of knowing exactly how to get involved. His conscience was cursing him. That was good, for he never wanted to give in to something so hideous without being deeply convicted about it. So what was next?

Three weeks had passed since he first met young Malachi. He had been reluctant to go back to the Bowery since the night he encountered the repulsive crowd at the boxing ring, but for reasons known only to God, Lee felt compelled to know the lad's whereabouts.

At mid-afternoon, Lee drove slowly through the City to the East Side and pulled to the curb at Hannigan's. He preferred coming to the Pub in the daylight hours since he was not a drinker of ale. *Grandmother always quotes a good one for this, thought Lee. Men love darkness rather than light because their deeds are evil.*

Only three non-evil men sat at the bar in the broad daylight. He took a stool at the end, not wishing to talk. He just needed to think. Not as though he had not spent hours on end thinking while at the newspaper, the presses humming, effectively blocking out any human voice. No one could engage him in conversation unless he stepped away.

Hannigan was at the pub.

"Hello, Payne," he said. "Irish coffee, hold the whiskey but burn it, heavy cream and sugar, a little nutmeg grate?"

"Exactly," said Lee. "How've you been, sir?"

"Fair," said the Irishman pensively. "I've thought a lot about y' since y' were here, hoping y'd return."

"Nice of you to say so, Mr. Hannigan. You seem a bit bothered today. Is something the matter?"

"I'm not sure."

"Is there any way I can help you?"

"Frankly, I haven't seen Malachi in a week, and he has never been away for more than two days at a time. I know he needs to work for food. I'm starting to worry about him. Maybe y' don't know it, but a lot of the immigrants are just found dead in the alleys with no one ever knowing what happened."

Lee jumped from the stool and reached for his coffee. "May I take the mug with me? You know I'll bring it back as soon as I can."

"Of course, but why would y' leave so quickly?"

"I'm going to find Malachi," said Lee. "I won't be back until I've got him with me. I've got to do it before dark, considering this place is terrifying when the sun goes down. Any ideas where he might be?"

"Try the boxing ring. He hangs out there sometimes."

"What?"

"Yes, he's fascinated by the fight, I think I told y'."

"I drove down there the other night by mistake. I don't know how it is in the daylight, but it's no place for men *or* boys after dark. I don't even remember how I got there. Can you tell me the closest route?"

"Cooper Union, Third Street past St. Mark's Place. Not far from here. It's pretty seedy over that way, so be careful."

"I found that out the hard way. Thanks, Mr. Hannigan. I'll be back, hopefully before nightfall."

Lee took the mug of coffee and left, trying to get this straight in his brain. *Malachi is taken with bare knuckle fighting? For heaven's sake, he thought.* He took a gulp of the hot drink and traced his route to the place of horror. Missing a couple of streets, he turned around and drove right to it. In the daylight it looked different. Quiet, with no vagrants in the alley, no loud and raucous noises, no dirty men coming out of the woodwork. Lee stopped his horse and sat a moment drinking his coffee. It was good, tasty and sweet. He was thinking of Malachi when the side door of the building squeaked open. And there he was. Lee was stunned. He called his name.

"Malachi!"

The boy broke out in a big grin and ran to Lee.

"Mr. Lee, Mr. Lee! What are y' doing down here?"

"I might ask you the same question, Malachi. This is no place for a fine boy like you. I've missed you, son, tried to find you at the tenements and at Hannigan's. He told me you might be here."

"He did?" Malachi was taken aback that Hannigan would know.

"Yes. He's been worrying about you. I'm surprised to find you here myself. Isn't this where they have the fights of a weekend?"

"Yes, sir. How did y' know that, Mr. Lee?"

"I drove through the Bowery looking for you about three weeks ago and ran into this place the night of the big fight. There was a lot of commotion. Sounded awful coming from that building you just stepped out of."

"It's always like that when there's a fight."

"Really? Tell me about it."

Malachi climbed aboard. He was dirty and smelly, reeking of the street and the filth of the boxing ring. Lee hoped he would be able to get the smell out of Oscar's carriage, but he felt compassion for the boy. He would worry about the carriage later.

"They let me do a little work down here from time-to-time. I need some clothes and shoes, and I'm trying to save up some money to get them."

Lee choked and sat there a minute before he could speak. "Where's your bicycle?"

"Oh, it's behind the building. Don't worry, nothing's going to happen to m' prized possession. Not ever, if I can help it."

"What kind of work do you do here?"

"I sweep and mop. The place is always filthy after a fight. I know I look a sight, but I don't have much of a place to clean up. Sometimes I go to the Custom House. They have some shower trenches. Only I don't have clean clothes to put on after I use the shower."

Lee sucked in another deep breath, trying not to be so obviously sickened. He couldn't stand this.

"Have you finished your job here for the day, Malachi?"

"Yes, sir."

"What about your pay?"

"I get that after the weekend, usually on Monday, such as it is."

"Can you go with me for a few hours?"

"Yes, sir."

"Get your bicycle."

Lee drove as quickly as he could, out of the Bowery and up Broadway taking the shortest route to Twenty-Third Street.

"I've never been up this far, Mr. Lee."

"You'll love it," Lee said, hoping the boy did not go into shock. "Have you ever heard of Stewart's Department Store?"

"No, sir. What's that?"

"A big department store is where they sell clothing of all kinds and sizes. They're tall buildings and they have elevators that take you from floor to floor."

Malachi was completely out of his world and his eyes were big as saucers. He knew nothing outside the Lower East Side, the Bowery. "I'm really not presentable, Mr. Lee."

"Don't worry about it, son. We'll take care of that, too."

Chapter

That was the Day—

It was the eighties, the beginning hopes of skyscrapers, builders begging for steel beams, struts and stanchion for the enormous structures in New York City. The majestic buildings must have elevators, ventilation, glorious steam heat and gas lighting and plumbing, water, and now electricity for lights and other meaningful opportunities. To Lee, it might be the best of times, because that—that was his calling. To build skyscrapers. He was trained and equipped, and it would be a grand profession.

The new multi-storied apartments for the middle class workers who took the rail and paid a nickel to get to work—were Lee's idea of good living. He would gladly give up horse and carriage for a clean rail ride with no worry about cooling and washing and currying a horse and cleaning a carriage and paying for stalls.

Still, hauntingly and in contrast, the Irish—tired and very poor and sometimes violent, packed into careening tenement buildings—were a dark and dismal contribution of a country that had emptied its failing walls and borders into the American scene and system. They sent their women with no comb or brush for coiffing a head full of disheveled hair, a dress or two with rips and holes conspicuously mended on the front when they could find a needle and a piece of thread. Friends from across the crowded way, who shared gossip and sometimes shouted to one another from the landing of a fire escape, surely would have been much happier and more comforted entertaining friends from a nice parlor and sofa. But that was never to be.

Lee drove slowly observing the melting pot, still thankful for the hills of Mississippi, no amenities of the eighties as New York middle and upper class enjoyed. But there were peaceful rolling hills and beautiful McGill Creek with its wall of soapstone on one side, and every tree and brushy bush known to the region offered up summer shade and comfort, on the other. In his mind, he felt the cold of winter; a campfire crackled by night, his grandmother rearranging the embers on the old brick fireplace to accommodate sweet potatoes for baking. The family drew near with the butter dish waiting anxiously for someone to test one with a fork. As the sweet potatoes dripped sugar, mouths watered, and the embers spit sparks onto the hearth. And—in the heat of summer—Lee remembered drawing many a cool drink of water from the deep well, and at night the only light was a million twinkling stars overhead, and a family-of-cicadas choir chirped until someone spoke and they stopped.

What a difference, what a contrast of cultures—the lonesome strains of Dixie and the blaring, raucous sounds of the Bowery Bands and street people. How could an American in his right mind choose one over the other?

Mr. A. T. Stewart's Department Store, *The Marble Palace,* with a front made of cast-iron and a glass dome skylight, was a remarkable emporium on the *Ladies' Mile,* and in the next few minutes, Lee would enter it for the first time, taking his new friend, Malachi, to purchase some brand new clothing. What Lee could buy on his slim budget, he was not sure, but as with everything else these days, it would come to him. He felt method and opportunity and hope in madness. He had good ideas about this, and it must be done one step at a time. He did not want to get ahead of his plan. He silently prayed.

> *Lord, help me. I need wisdom, physical and mental strength, and money. Please stretch my funds to cover what I must purchase this day. And forgive me for being a daresome soul. I don't mean to challenge you.*

Happy that he had picked up his pay envelope before leaving the newspaper for the day, Lee pulled to the curb of the *Marble Palace* and looked at Malachi. "Here we are, son. What do you think?" at which they both broke into great laughter.

"It is splendid!" shouted Malachi. "I've never seen the likes. It takes up almost a whole block."

"Well, let's get to it. We're going to purchase you some new clothing, and you must make the choices."

Lee could see that Malachi would not be able to speak a word for a few minutes. He had no control of the tears that filled his eyes. Lee could only imagine how he was feeling. He stepped across the threshold into a little room with a door that had magically opened and motioned for Malachi to follow him. They moved to the rear, both eyeing the beautiful wood-grain finish. The woman navigated from a built-in stool, starting and stopping and letting people off, letting people on. It was Malachi's first-ever elevator ride. In fact, he had never seen an elevator, neither had he given them much thought, though he knew about them. He never expected to *ride* in one, and he understood nothing about how it worked. Lee would explain without embarrassing him, waiting until they arrived and the door opened.

"We're getting off on the fourth floor, Malachi. The lady," he whispered, pointing to the corner where she sat on her perch, "will call it, and when she does, just move toward the door and step off."

Malachi, concentrating on his instructions, dared not speak, though each floor stirred his sense of taste and smell, a different fragrance of fabric and leather mixed with chocolate and toasted nuts of all kinds keeping him preoccupied until the ride stopped on the fourth floor and the door opened to an elaborate emporium, like an indoor bazaar of clothing and shoes and belts, undergarments, satchels and a million other articles which, when considered for a period of time, might cause one's mind to explode if unwary of what was taking place. Lee knew, at some point, Malachi would want to talk about the elevator, and he could hardly wait to hear what he felt and thought. He remembered his own first elevator ride at Gilsey House when he was Malachi's age.

"Let's look at trousers first and the choices we have. Short pants or knickerbockers? And we have to figure out your size by trying on some things."

"Knickers! I've never had knickers. Only short pants. Knickers would be splendid for when the weather changes. And much warmer."

Malachi was like a kid in a pastry shop. It all looked to suit him.

"Sizes and colors," muttered Lee. "Pants are mostly grey and brown and black." Malachi touched nothing. Lee understood he was embarrassed. This was going to take some focus and diplomacy, indeed.

When they had gathered an assortment of outer and undergarments, shoes and a belt, Lee moved to another area of the emporium and sought out a nice cotton knapsack for taking care of the new things.

"Now to try these on for size, Malachi. I'll stand right here outside the door and you go inside and try only the pants, shirts and shoes. Everything else will be okay. We'll try the belt last."

Skeptical about all this, Malachi took the clothes and stepped into the trying room. He came out with the gray knickers and a plaid blouse of red, black and grey, neatly tucked, the black shoes—and gray socks to the knees, which Malachi could not resist.

"That's a fine look, Malachi! I am so pleased. Don't you think the size is just about right? You're much larger than I thought. You look more like a boy of fifteen than thirteen."

"I could be wrong about m' age."

Lee cleared his throat again. This had been an affecting experience, almost heartbreaking, one that he would never forget, nor would he want to. To be able to do this for Malachi was just the grandest thing that had ever happened to him.

"Now, take those off and try the short pants and blouse. I think we need to get a pair of shoes that will be suitable for work. You don't want to ruin those good ones."

They tried it all then picked another pair of short pants, a shirt and some brown work shoes and short socks.

"Let me take that knapsack back."

Malachi, hoping to disguise his disappointment, handed Lee the bag. He was sadly giving up an amenity he had never before owned, but he would not have made Lee feel bad—not for the world. They went to the cash drawer to pay.

"Just a minute, I want to get a leather bag instead of this cloth one. It will last longer."

Malachi drew in a deep breath and gave the loudest sigh. "Mr. Lee, you can't do that, can you?"

"Yes, Malachi. Yes, I can. How do you like this nice brown one with a wide strap that goes across your body? That way when you travel on your bicycle, you won't lose it."

"This is much too fine, Mr. Lee."

"I don't think so, Malachi. I don't think so."

The boy was beside himself with joy. He had never owned anything so extravagant, nor had he seen such.

Lee swallowed hard, trying to suppress his emotions, incapable of speech in the moment. He couldn't look at Malachi, fearful of breaking down. Instead, he thought of Grandmother Rachel, who for years made the clothing her boys wore until they went to war and even then, they sent letters home, 'Mother, I need you to make me a pair of trousers. Mine are worn to the skin.' He could see his father, Albert Henry, running through the brambles and thickets of the Virginia countryside, snagging briar-covered twigs, tearing his flesh as they pierced his worn-out trousers.

Lee cleared his throat and said, "Okay, now, there is one more thing we need to do today, Malachi."

"Yes sir?"

"You take half and I'll take half. Let's get to the carriage."

Malachi rode with Lee on the driver's seat, flailing about, anxiously looking back to make sure the packages, neatly wrapped in brown paper and tied about with twine, were secure in the carriage. Lee sought to calm him while Malachi secretly wondered where he was going to keep these treasured gifts.

"Before we go too far, I want to talk to you about something, and I want you to give it serious thought."

"Whatever y' say, Mr. Lee. I trust y' with m' life."

"I'm glad to hear that, Malachi, because I want to do something that may be the best thing that ever happened to you, but it would mean a dramatic change in how you're living. You would have to stop sleeping on the streets and you would have a nice place to stay for a long time, that is, until we can figure things out."

Lee had no way of knowing what Malachi was thinking in this moment. Since his mother died over six months ago, he had lived no place but on the streets of the Lower East Side, had slept on the fire escapes of the tenement dwellings, and had eaten scraps from some kind Irish or German mother's table or not at all. He had worked hard, but could get nowhere, nor would he ever be able to.

"There's a place called the YMCA which stands for Young Men's Christian Association, on Twenty-Third Street at Fourth Avenue. It was built in '69, just eighteen years ago. I've been there many times, stayed there when I visited the City on weekends whilst at West Point, so I'm familiar with how they do things. It's called the McBurney Building, named for the first chief executive of the YMCA, Mr. Robert Ross McBurney. They offer many things, including schooling if you're so interested. I want to put you up there for three months so you can feel like you have a home. I'll pay for everything, including your meals. It's not costly at all, and that's the least I can do for what I'm about to ask you to do for me. But, truthfully, Malachi, that's not why I'm doing it. And I know you have no idea what I'm talking about, but you will soon. First, I've got to know if you're interested in staying at, we'll call it— McBurney's. Irish and splendid, eh? You won't know until you've been there. If we don't get you located someplace off the streets, you won't be able to manage much longer. This will take care of a lot of problems for you. So let's go."

Malachi sat on the driver's bench with his head bowed. Lee hoped he was thanking God for this opportunity, but he couldn't be sure. He stopped the carriage on the street and said, "Don't think I'm going to leave you alone, Malachi. Let's see what happens and you'll know—in a minute you'll know— if this is the right thing for you. Then we will go to Hannigan's and tell him you're okay, and we'll have a Malachi milk and a burnt Irish and talk about it some more."

Malachi looked up and smiled. "I don't know how to react to such kindness, Mr. Lee. Please forgive me."

"That's okay, son. That's okay."

They climbed the steps to the first floor of the nine-story red brick building. Hopeful and grateful.

That was the day Lee Payne felt more like a father than a brother, and as for Malachi, it was a new beginning, a journey to a place he had never been. He remembered nothing of his native Ireland, and he had never known anything in America but the dirty, grimy tenement dwelling and the street. He had been called an urchin for all these years, scrapping and struggling just to make it from one day to the next, never having known life apart from poverty. His initial reluctance was a-kin to facing the unknown.

He stepped into the shower trench with a bar of soap and a clean towel, scrubbed the filth from his body, lingering under the warm water for as long as he dared, hoping it would remove the grime and oily stench from his pores. Lee retrieved the new clothing, shoes, and leather satchel from the carriage and waited in Malachi's assigned bunk room on the sixth floor. Wrapped in the towel and feeling like a new person, the boy trekked down the hall, hoping he was going in the right direction, his old and dirty clothes rolled into a ball, the two dollars from his bicycle exchange in his hand. Lee stepped out of the sleeping quarters.

"This way, Malachi. New underwear and socks first. And which of the short pants and blouses would you like to wear?"

"The brown pants and this blouse," he said, pointing to one that was a far cry better than anything he had ever worn.

"I like the choice on a fine Irishman," said Lee. "Do you have the key to your footlocker?"

"Yes sir."

"You will need to keep it pinned to your clothing somewhere. You must not lose it."

Malachi folded the rest of his new clothes and placed them with his Sunday shoes and leather satchel neatly into his footlocker, feeling much like Irish royalty, if there were such a thing. The smile was permanently fixed to his lips. He leaned over and shook his damp hair, dried it with the towel, and pushed the auburn curls firmly into place, then draped the towel across the iron rail at the foot of his bunk to dry. Lee wondered how long it had been since Malachi had used a real towel. Moreover, he wondered how long since he had a bed to call his own.

He smiled, so proud of this boy—this brother, this son. Whoever he was did not matter. In this moment he belonged to someone.

"Here, Mr. Lee, I want you to take this money and pay yourself back for some of my new clothes."

Lee took the money and pulled the satchel from the locker. "Put it in the bottom of your satchel, Malachi. It will be your emergency funds. Two dollars is a nice amount. And let's just toss your old clothes and shoes into the garbage can outside."

He retrieved the last surprise he had for Malachi and tossed it to him. "Here, son. Every fine Irishman deserves a Herringbone Irish Cap! I think this one will suffice to properly accent all your new things. I hope you like it."

Malachi caught the cap with both hands and slowly turned it, stepped to the common mirror and slid it onto his head, covering a mass of curls.

"It's the finest cap I've ever seen, Mr. Lee. I could cry a thousand tears of happiness." He threw his arms around his brother and did just that.

They took the carriage ride to Hannigan's, Malachi shaking like a leaf and Lee with the coffee mug in his hand.

"I hope Mr. Hannigan and Cavanaugh don't laugh."

"Let them laugh—we'll laugh with them. Isn't that what the Irish do?"

"Yes, sir!"

But—it was not that way. Hannigan cried when he finally recognized Malachi. Cavanaugh sucked in a deep breath and hugged the boy.

"Y' smell blimey great, Malachi!"

"I know. That was the best thing I noticed in a long time. And I feel blimey great, Cavanaugh! I think I'm a new man! And I have a new home, and a sleeping bunk, and more new clothes and a leather satchel and my red bicycle—"

"And the blimey-ist Irish Cap I've ever seen," said Mr. Hannigan.

Then Malachi burst into tears again as if holding back since his mother died last Christmas. He couldn't stop. Hannigan brought hot milk coffee and set it before him. Cavanaugh hovered, and Lee Payne thanked God for the richest blessing of his life.

Malachi snubbed and sniffed and finally was able to speak again. "And I have a brother who loves me with more love than I could ever imagine."

When things calmed a bit, the brothers sat at the bar drinking their coffee and re-living the experiences of the day. The elevator. Malachi had to know all about it. That was easy for Lee. For all the training he had, he could practically build an elevator sitting at Hannigan's bar.

"All skyscrapers and large department stores must have elevators," he said. "This is how it works." And he explained things that no one but an engineer could possibly know.

They talked about Mr. Stewart's emporium with more items to purchase than one could imagine, the new things, the leather satchel. A new home with a bunk and a place to keep his belongings.

"Belongings," said Malachi. "Such a nice word, Mr. Lee."

Lee thought it inappropriate to abruptly interrupt, but he had to do so. "Malachi, what were your parents' given names?"

"M' mother's name was Molly and m' papa's name was Cullen."

"Molly and Cullen O'Malley," whispered Lee, placing the names in his memory, not wanting to forget. "Molly and Cullen O'Malley."

"Guess you won't be coming here anymore, son?"

"Oh, no sir. That's not true, Mr. Hannigan. Mr. Lee talked to me about that, too. He doesn't want me working any place but y'rs, that is, if it's okay with y'. I can easily ride m' bicycle from Twenty-Third Street down here to Cooper Union. Any day that y' want me. I will be taking some schooling classes at McBurney's on certain days, too."

"Well, now, I am proud of y', Malachi. Y're a fine Irishman, indeed."

Chapter 6

Needle in a Haystack

Late July in the City was insufferable. Hot easterly winds blew across the River driven by the currents off the Atlantic Ocean making everything and everyone in its path miserable. The things going on in Lee Payne's life mirrored the season, like an attempt to navigate the tidal strait up the River against a fierce current. Lee thought about that day so long ago when he almost died on board a motorized trade boat, the pitch so strong in Hell Gate, the malevolent waters of the New York Upper Bay, Long Island Sound, and the Hudson River by way of the Harlem converging and crashing. Years later, he came to better understand the madness of navigating the tidal current in the East River. And even better than that, he came to know the Lord preserved his life that day for some specific and magnificent reason.

He had made somewhat of a plan, attempting to consider the paths he had taken and those of which he dreamed. When Malachi showed up on the Boneshaker that day, nothing was the same and never again would be. Lee was as happy about that as he had been graduation day at West Point and the hopes of marrying Charlotte. It was nothing short of a miracle, a plan of God. There was something sublimely rewarding about taking on responsibility for a suffering human being. But while gratifying, it was a deeply complicated ambition that could become as troubling as the crashing currents of Hell Gate and the East River. Malachi was just one of millions, but Lee understood he could not take on the millions. Others could. One by one. He hoped they would.

His job as a draftsman with the architectural engineer would not be ready until mid-January of the New Year. He thought of all he must do in preparation of that day and for his marriage to Charlotte. There was a stir in the City about Carnegie, Vanderbilt and Rockefeller. Lee would be on the periphery. He had no hopes or plans to ever become involved in the politics of building structures and bridges and tunnels in the largest cities in the world. He just wanted a simplistic life above the poverty line with the people he loved, away from the East End.

Lee left the newspaper having worked until mid-afternoon. He picked up speed as he drove south on Broadway to the Battery, pulled his rig to the curb at the Custom House and dismounted. He wiped the sweat from his face and stood in the breeze off the Atlantic waters for a few moments before entering the large receiving room. The herring gulls screamed above his head as if they knew him personally and approved of what he was about to do.

"Right this way, Mr. Payne, and have a seat. In case you've forgotten, my name is Francine Benoît. I'll come out to get you momentarily."

"Thank you, Miss Benoît. I wrote it down so I would remember."

She smiled and left the room while Lee's emotions were exploding inside of him.

In a matter of minutes, the young attractive Miss Benoît wearing a black suit with dark hair firmly wound into a bun and affixed to the back of her head, returned with a cardboard box filled with papers.

"I had no success in my search since you were here yesterday to make your request, Mr. Payne, but that doesn't mean a thing. We hope today will bring good results."

Lee took the heavy box from her and followed.

She turned into a side room with nothing in it but splintered old wood tables, each surrounded by four chairs of the same condition.

The room was packed, he guessed with immigrants, each looking for someone or some ephemeral jewel from the millions of alphabetical archives.

"We'll take this table here, Mr. Payne. You can just put the box on the end."

She sat down on one side and motioned for Lee to sit on the other. The room had eight large transom-topped windows, but no coverings, each pushed half-way open for ventilation. A brood of pigeons roosting on the sills below chattered and squawked as they watched the search begin.

"This may be highly irregular, Mr. Payne, but everything we do at the Custom House is highly irregular. We all look forward to the day when our filing system will become simplified and all-inclusive for each immigrant family. We try our best to keep all the information on each family together and in the same box, but you can see how difficult it is. There are just millions of them. Every case is different, every family, unique. I pulled the boxes with last names beginning with 'O', all Irish immigrants, for our search. I finished three boxes of this size yesterday and this morning. There are many more. I wanted you to help me look through this box as I have reason to believe this may be the one, according to the dates on the outside of the box. I know how passionate you are about young O'Malley."

Lee was shaking. He was in his mid-twenties, born during the War Between the States, and had lived a lifetime over the past few years. He thought his life was prioritized, but suddenly a young urchin of an Irish boy crossed his path and—

God can change the course of rivers if he so desires, he thought, and satisfied the plan now belonged to Him alone, Lee would try not to mess it up.

"Mr. Payne, these papers are packed into the box in no good order. We're essentially looking for the manifest with the O'Malley's names on it. If we find it in this box, their papers should be in here, also. Of course, there could be a thousand O'Malleys. That's a common Irish surname. So, take a stack out and start searching. Maybe we'll get the luck of the Irish today!

"We know it has been at least twelve years, if Malachi was two years old when they arrived, so we're looking for dates somewhere around the year 1872, stamped in black ink. It will be best to look at every single piece of paper and stack to the side any that do not pertain to Malachi and his family. This may take longer than three hours, and if it does, if you can return tomorrow to continue, that will be splendid."

"I can return," said Lee, thinking he could come soon after he checked in at the newspaper and arranged for one of the boys to do his proofing. He had never asked off for any reason.

"I will be leaving you alone, Mr. Payne, to finish checking out for the day. I should return at half past four, and we close our doors at five, so keep that in mind as you will need to pack up what you've done and leave the balance for tomorrow. When I return, I'll bring another box for you to store the documents you've looked through."

Lee took his handkerchief and wiped the sweat from his face. He hoped so much to find the O'Malley papers today. *Malachi has no idea what I'm doing, but had he not said something to the effect that he was entirely willing for me to run his life?*

By four o'clock, Lee had gone through countless stacks of Irish immigrant papers, about a third with the surname O'Malley. He hoped he had not missed Molly and Cullen and Malachi. At a quarter past four, he placed them all into the empty box Miss Benoit had brought and continued searching the papers that were left while he waited for her. He had just half an hour before the doors would be closed and locked for the day. He would look through a few more and start over tomorrow.

And then his eyes fastened on an unfamiliar paper. It was a list, and at the top these words were written—*Manifest for Alien Passengers*—

The manifest was to be his clue, and here it was. He searched through every line quickly thinking that there must have been a thousand immigrants on that voyage.

The O'Malley papers should be in this box.

And then—he silently shouted, his emotions on the edge of his skin. For there on the manifest were their names. The needle in the haystack. He had found it.

Lee Payne leaned back in his seat, caught his breath, tears poured uncontrollably down his cheeks, and he choked. He continued to search through the box for O'Malley … O'Malley … Cullen O'Malley, when his hand touched the first document.

His heart pumped so fast he was fearful of fainting. He drew another deep breath and sought to calm himself. *Jesus, help me!*

One after another he pulled out their papers—*Cullen Byron, Molly McSwain, and Malachi O'Malley.*

It looked like everything was together, at least the documents he most needed. He stretched trembling hands across the table, rubbed them together and tried to calm himself to get a grip on what was happening, but to no immediate avail. When he saw the names written in black ink—Cullen Byron O'Malley, age thirty-five, of Dublin, Ireland; wife, Molly McSwain O'Malley, age thirty; one son, Malachi O'Malley, age two—it was more than he was physically able to stand. He took out his handkerchief and tried his best not to make a fool of himself. There were people all around. He didn't know why he cared, why it mattered. What mattered was that he could show Malachi that he was truly somebody, a real person with real papers. He held the documents in his shaking fingers and searched for Malachi's birth date then laid them all out on the table and examined every word. September 25, 1868. Fourteen years old. The boy was fourteen. He would be fifteen in just over two months.

Everything was there, spread out before him—birth certificate, immigration papers, death papers of both his parents. His father died of tuberculosis on board the ship; his mother of pneumonia in New York City. Molly had died in the tenement dwelling and was cremated. Lee allowed the authorities had updated the immigration papers at the time of her death, which meant someone had been in this very box just seven months ago. Malachi ran when it all happened, not wanting to be placed in an orphanage.

It makes sense, he thought. I would have done the same thing.

Lee, still wiping tears to clear his vision, kept searching until he came across another document with Molly O'Malley's name at the top, and underneath was attached the same sort of document with

Malachi's name. They were the most authenticate and most recent of the O'Malley papers with the exception of Molly's death certificate. In large letters across the top were printed the words, *The United States of America Certificate of Naturalization*. Proof that Malachi and his mother had received their citizenship before she died. The date was September 25, 1872. Malachi's fourth birthday, and he had received his naturalization because he was the son of Molly O'Malley, his mother. He was not only a real person, but he belonged to the greatest country on earth.

Lee wondered if he knew. He would have been too young to remember. Had Molly ever told him? Suddenly, Lee could not wait to be the one to tell Malachi. But in the moment he was still in awe of the reality.

For Immigration to have found him they, too, would have been looking for a needle in a haystack. There were hundreds of thousands of Irish immigrant children living on the streets of New York City.

Lee still had to talk to the immigration people about his permanent intentions. And Charlotte—she would have to know and give her full consent. What young woman in love with a man, and in her right mind, would want to make such a commitment?

"Charlotte!" said Lee, not realizing how his voice projected in the massive room.

"I beg your pardon," he said, looking around at foreign-born people who were gazing at him expressionless. He doubted that they could have understood him anyway.

He kept the O'Malley documents out and waited the few minutes before four-thirty, when the lady in the black suit would return.

Why do all New Yorkers wear black, he wondered? Not everything needs to be morbid, especially in the summertime. Especially today! Miss Benoît might be of French descent, but she speaks flawless English.

When she returned, Lee made the most of the thirty minutes left.

"You've been amazing," he said, "and I do apologize for firing so many questions, but I know my time today has come to an end. May I see you tomorrow for at least one hour? I would like to bring young O'Malley with me."

"Of course. I know you work until mid-afternoon. How about three o'clock."

"Yes ma'am. That would be splendid, and thank you for all your help in making this possible. I'm happy to have found Malachi's records. It's sad enough to be homeless, but to have no account of your existence, especially later in life, could be insufferable."

"You're entirely welcome, Mr. Payne. I will keep these documents in an envelope, locked in my desk until you return and we will talk about what you are hoping to accomplish. Would you like for me to go ahead and request copies of these documents be written and authenticated? We have official stamps in the Department of Immigration now that suffice for proof of immigrant documents."

"That would be splendid," said Lee. "Is there a charge for copying?"

"No, Mr. Payne. We have employees who are clever and competent calligraphers and I will see that it gets done early in the morning."

"I continue to be thankful," said Lee. "Good night, Miss Benoît. Until tomorrow at three o'clock."

A Custom House attendant, fittingly dressed in black, began to usher the remainder of the people out the doors. Lee thought of the life-changing documents that would be hidden away in Miss Benoît's office and decided he was exceedingly glad that someone, probably dressed in black, would be closing those huge windows and locking the doors to Custom House.

Early the next morning Lee sat at his grandmother's desk at *The Elite Press,* deep in thought of the past month. He picked up his tablet and turned the page, took his quill and dipped it into Rachel's inkwell.

My dearest Charlotte,

A lot has happened since I last wrote, and I have heard nothing from you in the meantime. I will not venture to think of all you are accomplishing as it concerns our wedding and future life together. Hasten the day! Which is only a little over five months from now. I know you will think in a complex manner, but actually keep it natural and as unpretentious as possible. As we get closer to the date, I will rent one of the new apartment dwellings on the trolley line. We can have the wedding in New York and your dear mother can come here and stay during that time. Think about The Central Park for the ceremony if you would like. Or the Brick Church. If you choose The Central Park, all we will need is a beautiful dress for you and wild flowers! The birds will sing for us. Think of it like when we 'collided in ecstasy' on the Brooklyn Bridge the day it first opened for traffic, the day I placed the ring upon your finger and we pledged our love to each other. It is etched in my memory as the supreme moment of my life.

I have attempted to fill my days with many activities, not just to pass the time, which is happening as we live and breathe, but to fulfill my desire of becoming much more of a human being than ever my thoughts have allowed. Sometimes I have a lower opinion of myself, thinking me to be selfish and loathsome. I'm trying to rise above myself and think of others. I have had a good life. When I think of how narrowly I escaped the war years except for the great losses I suffered in family members— and you experienced the same—I want to find ways to give back some of me.

The Lord has blessed and I have found a very significant way to thank Him. I must tell you, but 'twill have to be while I am looking into your face, for it concerns you as well as me.

If possible, I would like for you to come to New York for three days and nights in early September when the weather starts to cool a bit. I will reserve a room for you at Gilsey House and take care of your expenses, of course.

Come on a weekend so we can go to the Brick Church, which is Presbyterian. I know you are Baptist, like me, but I'm sure you will be agreeable since our beloved Stonewall Jackson was the staunchest of Presbyterians. This is the church where Rachel and Mr. Oscar attend, the one I have told you so much about, where the resurrected Christ is supreme. I understand three days is not much time, but I must work on the week days, and I know your job at the Mercantile will be waiting for you when you return. Also, two days will be taken with travel, so that will be a total of five days barring no delays on the trains.

I will wire your rail tickets and some money for expenditures in two weeks. I long to see you and hold you in my arms, dear Charlotte.

Oh, and we can shop for your dress at the *Ladies' Mile*, if you like. I promise not to look as you choose, but I will happily pay for the dress and longingly wait to see it, but, of course, not until our wedding day.

Your loving fiancé,
Robert E. Lee Payne

The presses awaited Lee and his thoughts of Charlotte and Malachi. He began to proof the copy in preparation for the printing of the daily news. The technique, much like that of an architect drafting blueprints for a skyscraper, would always amaze him. Before he realized it, his thoughts, like the wind under the wings of a herring gull, had propelled him through the early part of the day.

Chapter 7

Shock and Antipathy—

Lee drove to the City Hall Post Office and purchased some two-cent stamps. He placed one on his letter to Charlotte and dropped it in the monstrous slot for outgoing mail. His eyes fell on the elaborate architecture, thinking that the post office was the ugliest building in New York City. He stood in the center of the exhaustingly over-sized room and turned around slowly, surveying the structure from a hopeful architect's point of view. He much preferred more urbane, less Gothic in comparison. He wondered if he would ever be called upon to help design or construct a building with flying buttresses and pointed arches, grotesque and eerie. He hoped not. The visit left him with one question. Why did it take such a large edifice to house a few two-cent stamps?

He switched his horse and clopped through the streets to the simplistic but beautiful red brick building on Twenty-Third Street where Malachi would be waiting for him on the steps. Three weeks had passed since they made plans to meet at twelve o'clock noon on this day, and Lee had not seen him at all, nor heard from him, which was not unusual. There was really no way to communicate except by meeting personally. Lee was on pins and needles to hear if Malachi was adjusting, if he had started classes, if his new clothing was sufficient. He needed to talk about so many things, not the least of which was the fact that Lee had found Malachi's immigration papers.

And there he sat probably impatiently waiting.

"Mr. Lee, I have some really good news that y'll like. Did y' know that the McBurney has Bible study and prayer for the men? I get to participate every Thursday night. I have a lot to tell y' about Genesis. Y' won't believe it! They gave me a Bible. I'm so proud of it.

"I've been here three weeks and already I've started schooling classes, which I have never had. M' mother taught m' to read and write, but everything else—I learned on the street. Now I am in class at least three hours every day, and I do love it. I thought it would be impossible, but I have a good teacher who tutors m' in everything. I'm taking grammar, trying to learn to speak proper English without the Irish accent, mathematics, and history. When I finish those, I will start on the next subjects, whatever that may be.

"Oh, and I use m' satchel, which is now m' 'book bag'."

"Malachi, it looks like God is directing your life, and I'm so proud for you. But there's just one thing—"

"Yes sir?"

"It's the Irish brogue. Please don't lose it. Your Irish accent is why I like you so much!"

"That's funny, Mr. Lee! Okay, I'll likely keep most of it. But y' must know, I don't really like m' accent, especially m' pronouns. I've already promised m'self to work on those. I hope y'll see a difference soon."

"If you insist," said Lee. "Now, can we celebrate with food?"

"Oh, yes! I seem to always be starving lately. I've been working out in the gym when I can, and I ride m' bicycle to Hannigan's three times a week."

"Then, let's go to Mr. Oscar's favorite restaurant—Delmonico's! I think you need a steak for energy."

"I've never been to a restaurant except Hannigan's. I won't know what to do."

"You don't have to do anything. Just watch me a couple of times, and you'll soon learn. I did it by watching my grandmother. She did it by watching Mr. Oscar. We all have to have teachers before we can learn to do the proper things."

"Well, I got the best!"

Malachi was dressed properly in his knickers and the white blouse, knee high socks and his new black shoes. He looked and smelled like a fine gentleman. And Lee could tell he felt proud to be going someplace proper wearing his new clothes.

He placed their order, Malachi listening and watching so he would one day be able to do the same.

"Y've noticed, Mr. Lee, that I get all fidgety when I'm excited or nervous."

"I have, indeed, and that's pretty much the way we all do it, Malachi. I wouldn't worry over it."

"Oh, I'm not worried over it," he said. "But it must be annoying to y'. I've been trying to work on that, but there has been so much excitement in m' life over the last few weeks that I find it a chore to keep from it."

"Then don't concern yourself. I might be disappointed if you weren't excited over these things that are happening. I'm about to break some news to you that will either cause you to jump out of your skin in shock and antipathy, or you will be happy about it."

Malachi leaned across the table and said, "Mr. Lee, what does 'antipathy' mean?"

Lee laughed and said, "I used shock and antipathy together meaning that you would be shocked for sure and definitely opposed. Now that's pretty much positive on the negative side." He laughed and Malachi was ready with a reply.

"Well, if it's positive *and* negative, it can only be half bad, right?"

"You've got me there, Malachi."

They both tried to stifle any vociferous laughter.

"We should probably get ourselves under control or they might want to toss us out of Delmonico's, and 'tis only m' first visit."

"True," said Lee. "Then I should just tell you what I'm talking about and see how you react."

"I agree to that," said Malachi, attempting to act and look refined.

"Now, this is really serious, Malachi, though you might have to laugh at first. You remember when I told you about getting lost in the Bowery, way down on the Lower East Side the night I was looking for you?"

"Yes sir."

"I didn't tell you everything. I left my rig on the street, which was a really bad thing to do, but I let my curiosity get the best of me. To tell you the truth, I wanted to find where the bare knuckle fighting takes place, and something told me it would be in that part of the City. Truthfully, I was looking for you, but I got lost and it got darker and darker, and when the evil night unfolded and brought its wickedness out of the alleys and onto the street, I knew I was in a bad place. To be honest with you, I was afraid.

"When I think that you had been working down there and I saw what it was like, well, quite frankly, it made me sick. But that's over, now, so we don't worry about things that are past. At least, we shouldn't. Anyway, I heard all this shouting and yelling, actually yelping, more like a dog than a human being. I made inquiry about that and some low-life was obliged to tell me. He said there was a 'biter' in the ring, and his opponent was yelping because it was just the most horrendous thing in the world for someone to take a big plug out of another human being. I am sickened as I think about it."

Malachi intently listened to Lee without changing expression, and he didn't laugh. It was not something new to him, neither was it funny. He had seen it all. But why was Mr. Lee telling him this. Shouldn't he just be forgetting about it? After all, it was in the past.

"I know you're wondering now, Malachi, but it's important to me. You see, I'm in a dilemma. One of my own making, and if I don't do something to correct it, I won't be able to marry Charlotte anytime soon, neither can I get an apartment on the rail line, nor would I be able to purchase food for a while. You see, I start my new job in a few months. It's all arranged and I've signed my contract, but it will be that long before I can start making enough money to support a wife.

"I wouldn't be telling you all this, but you came into my life at a time when some changes are going on, and … well, I have to tell you, so here it is. I had this idea of trying to get into boxing—temporarily only, that is. I certainly wouldn't want to do it for very long. I might get killed as it is. But, Malachi, I think I can do this. I don't know what gives me the unction, since I'm not sure God is pleased with it, not a hundred percent; neither do I have any really bad feelings about it. I wouldn't be in it to kill some poor fighter. But I do need some quick money, and I just thought—well, I thought if you would get me in, so to speak, maybe I could try it out. I don't know how much influence you have, but if you would be willing to try—

"Have I gone off my rocker, jumped the rails? And do I see a smile on your face, Malachi?"

"No sir—actually, yes sir! I think 'tis amazing that y', as proper and gentlemanly as y' are, would be willing to do such a thing. Y' must love Miss Charlotte a lot."

"That I do, Malachi. Very much. You see, I purchased her engagement ring at Tiffany's, paid cash out of my pocket, and because I do love her so much—I spent far too much money, never stopping to consider how it would put me behind. It was a failure on my part to think everything through judiciously.

"You know, I do have a good job at the newspaper. I make a fair amount of money, but not enough to take a wife. In the future, my real job will take care of everything, but that does not help me now in preparing for a small wedding, a place to live, and food for the table. Does that make sense?"

"For what it's worth coming from me, someone who has lived on the street all his life, I'll have to say—yes! I think it would be splendid, and it would definitely be humbling, not that y' need to be humbled. But to be doing this for someone y' love, although I think she would hate it, well, it leaves me without words. And, yes, I know I can get y' in. Wait! There's just one thing—can y' bare knuckle fight?"

"Well, no—"

"Don't worry about that," said Malachi. "But listen, bare knuckle boxing will take y' to the ugliest side of life. I'll tell y', and I'll try not to leave anything out. Y' must be prepared for the aw'flest things you could ever imagine. Y'll have to know how to avoid certain things, like the biting y' wer' talking about. I can't say in words everything y' need to know.

"I think y've got to stand at ringside and just watch. Watch to learn. Rarely is there more than one fight on a night, and sometimes they go on and on until someone gets kill… Sorry, Mr. Lee, that's just an expression. Nobody hardly ever gets killed. It just looks and sounds like it, and they fight on and on and on trying to, let's say—win."

"Malachi, you are more than honest about this, and I thank you for that, even if you are making me feel like the worst sort of coward."

"Y' need to know, and m' best advice is that y' watch the fighters, pick y' best moves, and make y' decisions. I know this sounds crazy, but I can help y'. I've watched it all. I know what the best fighters do to keep from getting viciously attacked by a set of sharp teeth, and I know what y' need to do to avoid the hard blows to the face and head. We could even spar together and I'll show y' a few moves. I'm no boxer, but I actually think I could be a blimey-good trainer from what I've seen. It's vicious, Mr. Lee. It's wicked and vicious."

Lee sucked in a deep breath, feeling sick that he was involving Malachi in the evil art of boxing. Or was Malachi now involving him? This whole thing was crazy, but he was getting too deep into it to think about the implications. There was no law against prize-fighting, just some of the inscrutable methods; neither should there be any disgusting afterthoughts. He certainly hoped not.

"Oh, and by the way, Mr. Lee, there is a gymnasium at McBurney's, if y' remember. I can find some boxing gloves, I'm sure. And I'm almost certain I've seen a sparring bag. And sometimes the boxers do use gloves instead of bare knuckles. Y' don't really get to choose what y' want to do when it comes to the fight."

Lee was feeling a little better. Malachi was giving the impression it was somewhat civilized. Nothing said he would have to do the insane things some of the bare knuckle fighters were doing.

The two sat at Delmonico's eating sumptuously. It was not only Malachi's first visit to a restaurant, but it was the first steak he had ever tasted.

"Well, what do you think, Malachi?"

"I don't have words to describe how delicious this is," he said, pointing his fork to the last morsel of steak. "And, thanks for showing me how to cut and eat it. I'm beginning to think I'm a learning machine. I've so much in m' head."

"Well, now that you are almost finished with your steak, I think I will pile one more bit of information into that brain machine of yours."

"What more could there be, Mr. Lee?"

"This might be the most important piece of knowledge you've received in a long, long time, Malachi."

"Okay, let's have it. I think I'm ready."

"Actually, I think I'm just going to take you to a place you're already familiar with and show you."

"Where's that?"

"The Custom House down at the Battery."

"The Custom House? I only go, that is, I *went* there from time to time to use the showers. I haven't been back since I've been at the McBurney."

"How long has it been since you were inside the big waiting hall?"

"Not since m' mother stood in line with me the day we arrived from Ireland, as far as I know. I don't even remember it. I was but two years old."

"Well, there's a nice lady waiting to talk to us when we arrive. We will have an hour with her and she'll explain everything to you."

Chapter 8

There is a Place by Me—

Feeling somewhat apprehensive, Lee pulled to the curb at the Custom House, a place that was becoming familiar to him. He had done all the work, but what if he had overstepped his bounds in assuming that Malachi would approve.

"Should I be afraid, Mr. Lee?"

"No, Malachi. Why should you be afraid?"

"Because when m' mother died last Christmas, the immigration people came to get her body. They always do when someone dies in the tenements, and if there are children left with no parent, they take them away to an orphanage. I ran. Never was I going to an orphanage. There wer' awful street stories about such a life. So, like I said, I ran and just hid for days until I could think things through. I thought a lot, but nothing ever came to me. The days turned to months, and I was as lonely as any kid could ever be. M' mother was all I had, so I had to do m' grieving in the back alleys of the Bowery. I cried a lot, but finally I squared m' shoulders and tried to become a man. I found Hannigan's to be a safe place for m' to at least sort of hide out. Y' know? A regular place. At least someone would know where I was most of the time. That was seven months ago. Believe me, I have re-lived too many nights of sleeping on fire escapes and in dark alleys. I knew m' way around the Lower East Side, and I made enough at Hannigan's to survive with the help of some fine immigrant women who also live in poverty. They like to feed the street urchins if they have anything left."

Malachi chattered non-stop, crying the whole time. Lee choked back his own tears and managed to speak.

"I figured that out, and I don't blame you. I would have done the same thing. Malachi, do you remember not too long ago, you were learning about Moses' relationship to God? The book of Exodus?"

"Yes sir, I remember every word of it."

"Then this will be easy for you. Chapter 33 is all about Moses' desire to see the face of God. In essence, he was asking God for just a little more. I think Moses desired a closer fellowship with God and he thought if he could see Him face to face, it would be much easier. Maybe he wanted to humanize God. But God is much more than Moses could ever imagine.

"Well, God knew Moses. Knew him by name, and He said, 'Moses, you can't look on my face and live … but listen, Moses, *there is a place by me'*. I get chills when I think of how amazing that is … *there is a place by me.* Malachi, what on earth could be better than to be in that *place by Him*?

"So he told Moses to stand in the cleft of the rock and He would cover it with His hand and pass by. He did. And Moses saw God's glory. Malachi, don't answer this question right now. At least, not to me. Have you found that place God is talking about? Have you found the cleft in the Rock?"

Malachi did as Lee said. He didn't answer. He just kept crying.

"Right now, you need to know that you have a place by me, son. I know I'm not God, but I'm your friend that sticks close like a brother, and you can trust me. Do you believe that? You can answer *that,* Malachi."

"Yes sir. I know that. I know I have *a place by you*. Y' *are* m' brother."

"Well, Malachi, what we're about to do is something miraculous as I see it. And it's nothing like the old street life. You're all settled at the McBurney, and I've informed the immigration people that I'm taking full responsibility for you, for the time being."

"Are y' sure, Mr. Lee? Because I can disappear again. I know what to do."

"Is that what you want to do, Malachi?"

"Oh, no, I wouldn't wish that on m' worst enemy. Street living is dreadful. I have never in m' life had it as good as I do now, thanks to you, Mr. Lee. I love m' life now."

"Well, I promise you, Malachi, it's going to get even better. Now let's go inside. And, by the way, son—you look like a fine Irishman today."

That brought a smile to the boy's face, which was what Lee was hoping to achieve. He could hardly wait to see that face when Miss Benoît brought the papers to the table—

But instead, she greeted them in the large receiving room, introduced herself to Malachi, and escorted them down a long hall to another large room where many immigration workers took space together. It was a little more properly furnished with the same wooden pieces, just fewer splinters. The humming sound of combined chatter from all corners of the room would make it impossible for one table group to know what the other folks were saying. Theirs would just be a few more blending voices among a throng of people.

"Malachi, you sit here," she said, motioning to the chair across from her over-sized wooden desk.

He removed his treasured Irish cap and hung it on the chair, hoping he would not forget it.

"Mr. Payne, I'll ask you to slide a vacant chair over next to Malachi's.

"It's so nice to meet you," she said. "Especially under the circumstances. I'm sure Mr. Payne has told you everything."

"No, ma'am. He hasn't told me anything yet. Just that we wer' coming here, and that he was taking responsibility for me—for the time being."

Lee sat the chair down next to Malachi and said, "I thought it best to let you tell him, Miss Benoît."

"Well, we can just tell him together, Mr. Payne. How will that be?"

"I'd like that very much, ma'am."

"Tell me what? It must be good or y' wouldn't be smiling."

"Oh, it's good, Malachi," said Miss Benoît. "At least, I think it is. I'd like to do this by asking you some questions first. May I?"

"Yes, ma'am."

"How old are you Malachi?"

"I think I'm nearing fourteen, but I'm not sure."

"Do you know your birth month?"

"Yes, m' mother made sure of that. I was born on September 25, but I don't know the year."

"That was a great answer!"

Lee knew by now that Miss Benoît was confirming that Malachi was who he claimed to be. She only had Lee's word, and she was mandated by the authorities to get as much information as possible.

"Can you tell me your parents' full names?"

"Yes. Cullen Byron O'Malley and Molly McSwain O'Malley."

Miss Benoît smiled, knowing by now that Malachi was for real.

"Just a couple of more questions, son, and these may be difficult. They may sadden you, and I'm sorry … are your parents living?"

"No, ma'am. They're both dead."

"How did your father die?"

"I don't know the reason, but he died on board the ship when we wer' coming to America. He was sick before we left Ireland, mostly coughing all the time and very weak."

"Where is he buried?"

"In the sea. They buried him in the Atlantic Ocean."

At this Malachi was overcome with thoughts of how it had been, having grown up knowing his father never made it to this Country, and his poor mother having to live with it every day of Malachi's life.

"And your mother, Malachi. How did she die?"

"She took pneumonia this past Christmas. I knew it was bad and that she was hurting. She kept holding her chest and coughing. At first

I thought it was the same thing m' father had. M' mother told me how, even before we boarded the ship, m' father used to cough so hard he would lose his breath. There was nothing I could do, but I never left m' mother's side except to run next door and tell Mrs. O'Connor. She got a doctor to come and look at her. He's the one who told me she had pneumonia and that I should expect the worst.

"She just kept getting sicker. I gave her water and kept her warm. She wouldn't eat anything, even though we had nothing much to eat, only what Mrs. O'Connor shared, but she was as poor as we wer'. When I knew she was gone, I kissed m' mother's cold face and waited a few minutes then covered it with a sheet and blanket.

"I ran next door and told Mrs. O'Connor m' mother was gone. I asked her to get the police, and I guess they called Immigration because we wer' living in the tenement and we wer' not yet citizens. That's all I knew to do."

Miss Benoît had not expected Malachi to go into detail, but she let him talk and cry. She wiped her own eyes and attempted to get her emotions under control. She excused herself and was gone a few minutes.

Lee wiped the sweat from his face, leaned toward Malachi, and spoke. "I didn't know about the questioning, son. I hope you don't mind. I think it is something the Immigration Department does when they find one of their lost children. I'm not sure, but everything is going to be fine. I assure you of that. You did a grand job of holding up under all of this emotional drain."

She sat the hot cup of tea on the table for Malachi and added cream and sugar. "I don't know how you like your tea, Malachi, but you have definitely earned some cream and sugar."

"That's just the way I like it, Miss Benoît."

"Now, let me thank *you* for doing such a splendid job of answering my questions. You see, those were the answers I needed to confirm that you are really *the* Malachi O'Malley. Now I'm positive that you are, and because of that, I'm able to give you the good news.

"Actually, I'm going to let Mr. Payne give you the news, because he has done so much work on this and you need to know, this gentleman loves you very much and wants only the best for you."

"Yes, ma'am. I definitely know that." Malachi nervously pulled at his hands. He looked toward Lee for further approval. Lee gave him a reassuring nod, knowing that Malachi was having *a conniption.*

She reached in her drawer and took out an envelope and a small box. She handed the envelope to Lee and motioned for him to open it.

"Mr. Payne, if you will just explain each piece to Malachi ..."

Lee laid the pieces of paper in front of the lad and began to talk. "These are copies of original papers that some nice employees right here at Custom House made especially for you. They are all documented with a *Customs* stamp and you're going to take these with you. This first one is called a manifest. It's for those traveling for long distances, like across the ocean aboard a ship, which is what you and your parents did to get to America. You came in right here at New York Harbor with thousands of others from Ireland and possibly some other countries. See this line? Your name, your father's and your mother's. The writers have omitted all the other passengers' names to protect their privacy."

Malachi took one look at the paper and drew a deep breath.

"This is it, huh?"

"Yes, this is it, and these next papers are birth certificates and immigration papers for you, your father and your mother. And, Malachi, here are the death certificates of both your parents."

Tears streamed down Malachi's cheeks as he looked at the information concerning the passing of his parents. He knew the truth of it, of course, but seeing it on paper struck a poignant chord.

"How did they get all of this?"

"Well, Malachi, it's kind of like you belong to the Department of Immigration for awhile, at least they are responsible for you until you become a citizen, so when you come into the country, they have to get all this information on you. Am I saying that correctly, Miss Benoît?"

"Of course, that is a good way to explain it, Mr. Payne. Someone has to keep up with all of this information for many reasons. It would take too long to explain it all, but you will know more as you study in school and as the days go by, Malachi. Your personal information and that of your parents will forever be a part of our archives and you will always be able to access it as long as you bring your identification, which can be any of your documents. You are and have been a part of the history and heritage of America and the more you know of this amazing journey, the more you will understand your value as an immigrant to the greatest country on earth."

Lee picked up the last two pieces, his fingers shaking.

"Are you alright, so far, Malachi?"

"Yes, I'm really quite surprised and glad to know all of this. I actually feel like … for once in m' life … I'm a real person."

"Did you notice the year you were born on your birth record?"

"No, I guess I wasn't thinking about that."

"Here, take a look at it again," said Lee.

"September 25, 1872. Let's see. This is 1887. No! I'll be fifteen in two months?"

"Yes! You'll practically be a man in two months."

"Oh, my goodness, Mr. Lee. I will need to work hard to get prepared to be a man."

"You've already got that happening, Malachi. Education is a great way to become a man, among other things. You will see. You've already educated yourself on how to manage on a shoestring budget and how to live without a roof over your head. You've practically been at war just trying to survive these seven months. And now you're taking education classes at the McBurney. So I'd say you have a grand start.

"Now, one more thing, maybe two. Look at this document."

Lee laid out the Declaration of Naturalization certificate belonging to Molly McSwain O'Malley.

"What is this one?" asked Malachi.

"Read it, son."

"What! M' mother got her citizenship? That is blimey splendid! Oh, pardon me, Miss Benoît. I didn't mean to swear!"

Miss Benoit laughed out loud. "No pardon required, Malachi. In fact, that was a blimey good answer, if you ask me."

They all laughed.

"And here is the last paper, Malachi."

Lee placed the document in front of him and Malachi stood, slowly, reverently. It was the best thing he could do. He staggered under the weighty thought, his tall and lanky frame shaking. Tears streamed down his cheeks and he could hardly see, but he knew. He knew it was his naturalization paper. It was hand written in calligraphy, a beautiful certificate of his citizenship. He picked up the paper and caught his breath in an emotional moment.

"Is this mine to keep, and does it really mean I'm a citizen of the United States of America?"

"Yes, just like your mother was, son. I take it she never told you. You were but a lad, and on your fourth birthday, on September 25, 1876, while surely holding fast to her hand, you were sworn in as an American citizen because she was. That was the year America turned one hundred years old."

"I've never been so proud in m' life," said Malachi. He knew his strong Irish accent was conspicuous, but there was nothing he could do about it. "Thank y', Miss Benoît for all y'r trouble. I'll never forget y' for this. And, Mr. Lee, oh, Mr. Lee, what can I say to y'? Y've made m' the happiest street urchin in all of New York City. It will take the rest of m' life to repay y' for all the good y've done m'."

"Save a little rejoicing, Malachi, for there's one more thing," said Miss Benoît. "Something a little tangible that you will love. A memory or two, maybe three. Something even Mr. Payne doesn't know about."

She slid the small box across the table to Malachi. He pulled the old, dingy string and let it fall, then opened the box. His fingers shook as he took out two tiny American flags, and again the tears rolled down his cheeks.

"I'm not sure, but m' thinks these may be the flags they gave us when we swore in. I've seen the other immigrant kids with them after they got their papers. I always wished for one, thinking how grand it would be to receive one."

"That's exactly right," said Miss Benoît. "And there's something else."

She reached into the box and took out a tiny gilded-edged frame with a picture of his mother and father on their wedding day. Malachi pressed it to his heart and shook, trying hard to keep from crying aloud. "M' mother kept this beside her bed always."

Miss Benoît sighed and swallowed hard. She placed a small object wrapped in tissue paper into his hands and said, "One last thing, Malachi. Hold this over the table. You don't want to lose it to the wood floor."

He unfolded the paper, holding it gently over the table. There was a piece of paper inside that read, *last will and testament of Molly McSwain O'Malley.*

"The sight of m' mother's handwriting gets m' emotional." He read her words aloud, *"The wedding band on m' finger is for m' only son, Malachi O'Malley, with all m' love and all the life left within m'."*

"M' mother's gold wedding ring," he said softly. "I always regretted that I didn't take it off her finger the day she died. I cried about it for weeks. And here it is. I always loved this ring. M' mother knew it, and she would love that I now have it. That is, if it's mine to keep?"

"Of course, it's yours to keep, Malachi," said Miss Benoît. "When Immigration goes into the tenements after someone has passed away, if there is no surviving family, they look for any and everything that might be of sentimental value to a survivor. Of course, your mother was wearing the ring, but they found this note in an otherwise empty drawer and they knew—and they brought her personal belongings to the Custom House for safe keeping. That way, when miracles like *you* come along, they know what to do with them. If you still lived on the street, we would continue to hold the ring, but since you have a lovely home at the McBurney, you will have a place to hide it, I'm sure, or perhaps Mr. Payne can help you get a safe place for it."

With this, Malachi, still standing, walked around and put both arms around Miss Benoît, then he hugged Lee and—well, there was no more to be said. They had said it all, and Malachi would never be the same for it. He was now a real person with citizenship in a real Country, the greatest Country on earth, and he now had the sum of his mother and father's earthly possessions to call his own.

Lee pondered the moments of the day, thinking what an incredible young man, this Malachi O'Malley. There was nothing of value left in the tenement the day he ran except the flags, a photograph of Cullen and Molly O'Malley, and the gold wedding band that her son treasured. It was all Malachi needed.

How Lee wished Cullen and Mollie O'Malley could see the face of their handsome auburn-haired Irish boy on this amazing day!

Chapter

I'm Going to Die—

Lee allowed himself only a few weeks to prepare for the ring. It was a crazy thing to do. He knew that. But by now, he didn't have much choice. Charlotte would come early in September and he wanted to get at least a couple of fights behind him before she arrived.

"This makes a pretty nice boxing ring, Malachi."

"Yes sir. Don't get y'r hopes up for the one in the Bowery to look like this. 'Tis dirty and so are the people who hang around down there."

"Am I going to be sorry for this?"

"No sir. Y're just going to be humbled."

They laughed, tied the gloves on and started to spar.

"You're good, Malachi."

"Yes sir, and as for y'self, y' need a lot of work, begging y' pardon, sir. Let me show y' some moves to keep y'r opponent from even thinking he can lay teeth on y'. Y' may have to knock his teeth toward his throat. That's just the way it is.

"Now, I want y' to start punching this bag. Don't draw back. Before y' can get y'r arm back around, he'll have y' on the mat. Just short left-handed jabs. Short. Like this. And cover y' face with y' right hand. Higher. Close and tight with y' left hand and high with y' right. Tuck y' arms."

Malachi began to throw punches at the bag, doing what he had told Lee to do.

Lee thought, this little guy is amazing. Either he has been fighting or taking lessons. Neither was true. Malachi had been watching for a couple of years.

"M' mother used to wonder what I was doing in m' spare time," he said. "Besides, I love it. 'Twas glad I was to find out the McBurney has this place. Y're doing fine, Mr. Lee, just keep going. Y'll work up y'r own way of doing this. Not too much this first time, but y'd do well to come at least every other day for a couple of weeks."

"Remember I told you the day we purchased your clothes that I would be owing you before long."

"Yes sir."

"We'll go back to Mr. Stewart's Department Store to get you a few more things to wear. At that time, I had probably better visit their sporting department if there is such a place. What do these boxers wear?"

"I'd get some black shorts and a couple of white undershirts, a size smaller than y' actually wear on the shirts. How does that sound?"

"I don't wear shorts, but I guess I'll give in to that. And why do I have to get my undershirt too small?"

"Y' don't want to give y' opponent any room to grab y' shirt."

They laughed.

"And y'll need some boxing shoes. I don't know what they call them, but Mr. Stewart's store might have them."

When Lee returned in two days, Malachi greeted him with the news.

"Y' won't believe this, but I've got y' a match with a welterweight in two weeks, Saturday night."

"What?"

"Yes sir."

"What's a welterweight?"

"It's a boxer that's just about y'r size. I figure y' weigh in at about 146 pounds."

"How did you know that?"

"I guessed."

"You were close. I weigh 147."

"And that's exactly how much a welterweight weighs. Y'll get paid if y' win. If y' do a good job, they'll want y' back. If y' lose, y'll go home hurting and y' may not look too good."

"I can't afford to get my face all damaged. Charlotte's coming."

"I thought about that," said Malachi. "We better get busy. Y' need to get y' footwork down. Watch m' feet."

Malachi moved quickly and methodically, more like a dancer than a killer boxer. Lee watched carefully, hoping to be a quick learner.

After a couple of hours they called it a day and went to the steps of the big brick building.

"Tomorrow we'll go to Mr. Stewart's store. Will you be ready about four?"

"Yes sir. I have to be back in time for Bible Study at seven."

"You'll be back."

"Do y' want to go—to Bible study, that is?"

"Yes. Yes, I do, Malachi."

Two weeks passed quickly for Lee and Malachi and Saturday brought a lot of anxiety for Lee.

"It's a good thing you're keeping a level head, Malachi. I'm about to have a conniption."

"Y're funny, Mr. Lee. What's a conniption?"

"It's more or less an anxiety attack."

"Y' mean like I had at Custom House?"

"Exactly."

"Just breathe, breathe, and keep bouncing like I showed y' when y' get into the ring. Y've been learning a lot, and I think y're ready for this. Keep y'r chin down and cover y'r face with the right as much as possible. Left punches. Use every muscle in y'r body. I'll be right in y'r corner, just outside the ring. Y' won't get a break much. They want y' to fight till y' can fight no more. Be strong and think about Miss Charlotte. Y're doing it for her. Now—go do it, Mr. Lee."

Lee wasn't sure he wanted to think of Charlotte in this moment. She would not approve of this at all. In fact, no one Lee knew would approve of it. He closed his eyes for a moment and tried to pray, but he feared the Lord would not hear him. The scripture from II Timothy expounded in Malachi's Bible study group two weeks ago flashed before him.

> *I have fought a good fight, I have finished my course, I have kept the faith—I'm going to die, thought Lee momentarily, else why am I thinking of this verse. Either from anxiety or at the hands of a merciless bare knuckle boxer who has just entered the ring—I am going to die. Think, think Robert E. Lee Payne. Be a man. Think of Charlotte. Think of Malachi, who put his heart into this.*
>
> *Henceforth there is laid up for me a crown of righteousness which the Lord, the righteous judge, shall give me at that day—*

Lee vaguely remembered Malachi ushering him to the center of the ring where the official introduced the two men and gave them the rules of the fight. The fight—Lee was about to engage in the art of attempting to kill an opponent with hard blows to the head, neck and shoulders.

Shocked into reality when he heard the bell ring, he realized he was landing the first punch, then another, and another. His feet were moving with every beat of his heart. His left hand had become lethal and he covered his face with his right. He felt naked without the gloves, but he was in for the duration and he must *fight a good fight.*

There was no time to pay attention to the crowds that were yelling with highest intensity, no time to think about who had wagered what or how high the stakes. No time to smell the blood and the filth of the ring.

Malachi was spellbound as he watched Lee. He loved the idea that he was his manager. He tightened the beloved Irish cap and increased the decibels, in fact, to the top of his lungs he yelled instructions. Lee had all the trappings of a professional bare knuckle fighter. His opponent was not a vicious man, but he was a good fighter and he was strong.

What are the odds here, wondered Malachi? God help Mr. Lee is all I can say right now. The smell of the ring filled his nostrils. Oh, how he hated that part, the stench near unbearable. But, the raucous crowd apparently loved it, and the more blood that spurted, the louder they cheered.

In the eighth round, both men were bleeding from the face, liquid crimson dripping onto the mat. Lee could see well enough to know the opponent was tiring.

"Tighten up, Mr. Lee! Y' can do this!" Malachi yelled.

Obviously motivated by Malachi's plea, Lee gave a hard, quick punch with the left and followed it with a solid right and that was it. His opponent hit the mat face down in his own blood, and he was out cold, down for the count. The bell blared and the fight was over. Lee had won.

There was never a moment in his life when Lee Payne regretted having been a country boy, a southern hillbilly, raised in the woods of Calhoun County. And four years of avoiding the *Union* boys at West Point, who couldn't, for one moment let him forget who won the war, had driven him to the running trails through the woods for miles on end, rain and shine, snow and sleet.

It had all paid off in this one night of victory. He spent his moment with hands raised high by the officials, stepped out of the ring where

Malachi waited with a big white towel, and said, "Let's get out of here, fast, down the hall to the window."

He pushed Lee into the small room where the purser waited with his winnings in a burlap bag tied with course string.

"No time to count it, Mr. Lee."

"You're right about that, boy," said the purser. "Get out quick or you'll have hungry men hanging onto you for a hand-out. It's a pretty good bag tonight. So run!"

The two young men took the purser's advice and ran, tipped the valet, so to speak, and jumped aboard Lee's rig.

"Mr. Lee, y' don't look half bad. I think that cut on y' lip and ear will heal by the time Miss Charlotte arrives, but we need to get y' to the McBurney and let me clean it up and find some ice. Y're going to have to remember to cover y' face and y' ears a little closer."

"It's easier with the gloves," said Lee.

"You can say that again. I'll try and arrange a match with gloves next time. The man y' fought tonight hardly ever loses. I'm proud of y', Mr. Lee."

"I'm more shocked than anything," said Lee. "Malachi, you know I couldn't have won this fight tonight without your help. I can easily say you taught me everything I know about boxing."

"We did it together. 'Tis nerve wracking, but maybe worth it."

They sat in the carriage discreetly counting the money. Sixty-seven dollars.

"Sixty seven dollars, Malachi! Why that's a lot of money. If I can live through five fights, that will be all I need. I'll stop at that. I'm going to pay you for being my manager, but I'm going to keep your money in an envelope next to mine in a drawer at Grandmother Rachel and Mr. Alexander's house. There it will be safe, and I'll give it to you when you are eighteen. How will that be?"

"Y' don't need to pay me, Mr. Lee?"

"Yes, Malachi. Yes, I do."

"Then that will be fine. And, will y' keep m' mother's ring and m' immigration papers in the drawer?"

"I think that's a good idea."

"Let's go find some ice for y'r face and get this blood off of y' before somebody sees y'."

"It is embarrassing," said Lee. "But my worst nightmare is getting blood on Mr. Oscar's rig."

Chapter 10

Search for Higher Ground—

Lee sat at Hannigan's partaking of an Irish coffee, waiting for Malachi to finish his work. Weeks had passed since he had been there to see Mr. Hannigan and Cavanaugh. Furthermore, he wanted to give Malachi a ride to McBurney's. Lee and Hannigan bantered as usual when came the question Lee was expecting.

"So y've turned into a prize fighter, eh, Payne?"

"Somewhat, but not a hundred percent."

"Don't worry, I'll not spill the beans to anyone besides Cavanaugh. Malachi told me y're a blimey good fighter."

"He exaggerates."

"No. Malachi never exaggerates. He's just proud of y'."

"It's just a little experiment, sir. I definitely don't plan to make it a profession."

"Can't blame y' for that, but it is a good way to make some fast money."

"And that is my hope, Mr. Hannigan. Am I bordering on insanity?"

"No, not at all. I understand that part. You just be careful down there. It's a den of iniquity, I've heard."

"I dislike that part. That's why Malachi and I push each other out the door as fast as possible when a fight's over. I don't want anyone to know who I am and where I live, and I certainly don't want them hounding Malachi."

The side door creaked open and Malachi slipped in with his mop and empty bucket. He disappeared to the back and emerged empty-handed.

"All finished for the day?"

"Yes sir, Mr. Lee," he said smiling. "I've already washed m' hands."

Lee ordered a milk coffee for the boy and a bit of salami, creamy white cheese and crusty bread.

"Just what I needed," said Malachi, scarfing down the fine treat. "How did y' know, Mr. Lee?"

"I put myself in your shoes."

"I can't seem to thank y' enough for all y' do for me. Y've made m' to feel like that poor Mephibosheth who sits at the King's table forever."

"Bible Study, eh?"

"Yes sir. It's really good, Mr. Lee. I'm learning. In fact, I never dreamed there was so much to know about the Scriptures, and these gentlemanly scholars stick directly to the Bible. I watch and read right along with them."

"I'm so proud of you, Malachi and thankful for your good teachers at McBurney's."

"But I have some questions."

"I thought you would. I thank God for Grandmother Rachel, my mother, Cassie, and my father, Jonathan. They have always answered my questions. We will talk very soon about what you're learning and see what your questions are."

Lee knew Malachi had been thinking about his personal relationship with Jesus, whether it was for real, or whether he had even had a spiritual experience he could count on. One that would do when the worlds were on fire. He knew what he was getting at the McBurney, for he had been there. His Bible teachers were dedicated men of God, volunteering their time and knowledge to the young men of Lower Manhattan. They came, in large part, as a result of the Fulton Street Prayer Meeting and the Great Revival that took place in Lower Manhattan back in 1857 before the war broke out. Lee had come to know in his own life that conviction is a grand opportunity, and Malachi was sorting some things out in his mind and heart. He dared not put words in his mouth and thoughts in his mind. This was something Malachi would need to do on his own and Lee would help him when the time came, when the Spirit of God led him.

Malachi finished every crumb of the crusty bread and ate the last of the salami and cheese. They said their good-byes to Hannigan and Cavanaugh, boarded Lee's carriage and clopped away up Broadway to McBurney's.

"Malachi, I've already won three fights, thanks to you. I don't want to foolishly squander my good fortune of winning by a loss that would probably devastate me. That's the bad part of the gamble, although I'm not wagering money. Miss Charlotte will arrive the first week of September, and I want to have plenty of time to wipe the grin off my face from winning, and put on a real smile for her. I sound like an evil man, I know. But—I am doing this for her. If only I could think of it as a second job, maybe I would feel better—more like an honest man."

"Mr. Lee, I would like to help y' with that. There is no more of an honest man than y' are. I can't see that what y're doing is evil. It is sport. It requires the best of y' and the money is hard-earned. Think of it as no more than playing baseball for a team and earning money."

"But the money that is hard-earned, is it not from wagers against one man and for another, and are not the poor immigrants who have no money to spare wagering hard-earned dollars on a fight?"

"Y' got me there, Mr. Lee."

Malachi paused a moment and said, "We will just hope to be finished with all this soon and get on with living a better life."

A better life, Lee thought. I cannot even contemplate a better life for Malachi until this is over.

Lee read the Scriptures before turning off the light beside his bed—the electric light. Mr. Edison had done something magnificent for the people of New York City. The night had become amazingly brilliant, twinkling like the stars above Manhattan, sort of bringing heaven and earth together in one glorious display of light.

No man living, thought Lee, could do what our Mighty God has done. He systematically positioned the sun, moon and stars into place, and then He gave the likes of Thomas Alva Edison the brains and ingenuity to turn His awesome energy into something that could materialize at the flip of a switch upon the wall.

"Oh, God! May I never doubt your power and glory," he prayed aloud.

He thought of Malachi and thanked God that he was learning day by day. Soon—very soon, at God's timing, Lee would sit down on the steps at the McBurney and they would talk about eternal matters.

Just two more fights. Dared Lee pray for two more victorious ones. He trembled at the thought of it.

Chapter 11

The Long Night—

Lee and Malachi pulled behind the building that reeked with the filth of stale body fluids. They covered their faces and ran, though it was not much better inside.

"Malachi, I have a bad feeling about the fight tonight. I don't know why, but I do."

"I understand, Mr. Lee. So do I. And I don't even know y'r opponent. Just go in there and do what y' always do. Keep y' face covered as much as possible and use that left hand to try and stop him."

"Is it bare knuckle tonight?"

"I think so."

He didn't say it to Lee, but Malachi, upon observing the fighter, was afraid he was dirty, unconventional. He hoped not. He *prayed* not.

Lee stepped into the ring, his palms bound tightly. For some reason, he was not afraid, but he knew he was going to lose this fight and that his life was probably at risk.

Once again, he bounced to the center of the ring, touched the fists of his opponent and when the bell sounded, Lee laid into him. It angered the fighter from the start and Lee sensed that he had aggressively signed his own death warrant. The man pulled every dirty trick from his cache and unloaded on Lee. Before he knew what hit him, Lee slammed hard to the mat and after a few counts, he staggered to his feet. Thinking he was not quite ready to throw in the towel, he came back with his fierce left hand, twice, three times. His opponent reeled and hit the mat with a thud. Stirred again by anger, he managed to stand to his feet, railed against Lee, threw his leg out and tripped him, catching Lee off guard as he fell. Lee staggered and regained his footing. It was expected of him—to fight to the death. And what a terrible way to die. With the scream of an eagle, his opponent flew into Lee's chest and clamped down on his shoulder with a set of nasty teeth.

It was Lee's worst nightmare, and he screamed the all-familiar sounds of an amateur fighter caught in the grip of a merciless monster that would not let go, and like a lion with prey, he tore the flesh and blood flew everywhere. Malachi yelled instructions to Lee, but they fell on deaf ears. Lee had taken leave of his senses except those that triggered pain. He just wanted to get away from the vampire killer. He knew he had lost the fight.

But in a momentary rally, Lee caught a second wind, vowing though his opponent might win, he would look as bloody as Lee Payne when the fight was over. That is, with the exception of a hunk of flesh that was torn from his shoulder. Lee landed a few more hits, refusing to go down again, the last punch knocking a front tooth out. Blood gushed from the mouth of his opponent, just a little unintended gift of revenge from Lee for the damage to his shoulder. At twelve rounds, both Lee and his opponent were still standing, but both were finished. The judge would have to pick the winner from two bloody bare-knuckle fighters. Lee knew it would not be him. His shoulder was bleeding profusely where the vampire had torn the flesh, where he had sealed the fight, draining Lee of all impetus. But Lee had managed to keep him away from his face. He could hide the shoulder, although it would require repair with stitches and shots, he was sure, but he would not be able to hide a mangled face.

Lee retreated to his corner and stood, though in pain, thanking the Lord he still had all his teeth. Malachi was there with a cool wet cloth for the mammoth hole in his shoulder.

"Nasty, huh, Malachi?"

"A bloody mess."

Lee writhed in pain when Malachi touched it with the cloth.

"I know it hurts."

"I can't tell you how much, son."

"Well, y' did a blimey good job of hiding it, Mr. Lee."

"I felt like I was yelling my head off."

"Y' did a fair amount of yelling. We'll get out of here quick when the judge calls it. We've got to get y' to the hospital. Mostly for some shots, thanks to the mad dog."

"Can we go by Hannigan's and let me clean up first? That is, if we can enter by the back door so as not to be seen."

"I think so, but we need to hurry. The dog has taken a hunk out of y'r shoulder."

The referee brought Lee's opponent to the center of the ring, and shouted—"And the winner is—"

It was not Lee, and there was no time for remorse. He had taken the bitter with the sweet. He had fought and won. He had fought and lost. But this time there would be no victorious lifting of the arms for Lee Payne. Whatever lessons were due him, he had learned the hard way. He had but one fight left, and he would be finished. If he needed more money, he would have to figure out a more civilized way of making it.

What on earth would Charlotte think? She must never know. What on earth must the Lord think of him? Lee knew he could not hide from an omniscient God. Surely there was purpose in Lee's insanity. Maybe he would understand later.

At Hannigan's, Malachi cleaned up as much of the blood as he could and stuffed a clean damp cloth into the wound. Lee dressed without calling too much attention to himself. Cavanaugh knew what was happening and helped, and then they were on their way to Bellevue, Lee talking non-stop, attempting to distract from the pain. Malachi responded as best he could, wishing he could help more.

"You're doing a good job of driving, Malachi. How did you learn that?"

"By watching y', Mr. Lee. Remember, we learn by watching those we trust."

Lee managed a smile through the excruciating pain, hoping Malachi had learned by watching him in the fiasco tonight, and that he would never attempt such for himself. Just maybe that was the purpose for all this.

Malachi pulled the carriage into the busy emergency entrance drive and helped as the medics hoisted Lee onto a gurney. He parked the carriage and ran into the emergency room, begged the attending lady at the desk to let him go to Lee.

"He's m' brother," said Malachi.

The lady rolled her eyes and said, "Go ahead."

She smiled, doubting the lad was telling the truth. The accents didn't align one bit. But she couldn't help noticing the devotion of a young lad to someone who was like a brother. And to Malachi it was the truth. Lee *was* his brother.

Lee Payne lay as still as possible on the gurney, the emergency room doctor horrified at what he was seeing. Poor Malachi pressed his shaking frame against the wall, afraid that what he was about to see—if he had the stomach to watch—would be worse than the fight.

"This looks like a dog bite, son."

"Yes sir. It pretty much feels like one, too."

"Well, I'm going to treat it like it is one; however, I know what this is. Have you been prize-fighting?"

"Yes sir. I know—I've near lost my mind."

"Why are you doing it?"

"For the money, sir."

"I venture to say you didn't make much tonight."

"You're right about that."

"Well, after I get this cleaned up, I'm going to give you some shots right in the middle of it and if you think it hurt when the dog bit you, you will not believe how this is going to feel. Just giving you a little warning."

“Yes sir,” said Lee, understanding the doctor’s abridged lecture to be an admonition to stop the bare knuckle fighting nonsense. Lee gritted his teeth and prayed that he would not scream or moan.

Malachi leaned hard against the wall, turning gray from the sights and sounds. A nurse, predicting what would be next for the boy, escorted him out with some cold towels. As soon as he regained his gumption, he returned in time to watch the doctor stitch up his friend. He fought the tears and watched Lee’s knuckles turn white as he clutched the sides of the gurney. Within an hour the doctor announced that the stitching was done and he was about to give Lee some shots in his arm.

“These shots will help with the infection if the dog that bit you had any diseases.”

Lee knew what the doctor meant. Getting bit by a human could be as dangerous as getting bit by a dog.

“You got anybody to stay with you tonight? You’re going to need help if your fever goes up.”

“Malachi?” Lee whispered as he lay trying to regain his composure.

“Yes sir. I’ll stay with you, Mr. Lee.”

The night was long. Lee Payne lay dying in his bed—at least that is how he felt. The memory of the fight added humiliation to the excruciating pain in his shoulder. He wanted to pray, but words wouldn’t come. He was embarrassed, reluctant to approach the Throne of Grace with his foolishness.

Malachi never asked what he could do to ease the pain. For some incredible reason, the boy, full of street instincts, always came up with the right thing to do. He boiled water on the kitchen stove and poured it into the magnificent claw-foot tub, alternated with two clean white cloths he found in the linen closet. The warmth was soothing to Lee and temporarily eased the pain that extended from the heart of the wound to his entire shoulder and arm. Malachi carefully measured two capfuls of laudanum and gave to Lee.

"Y'll be asleep in a few minutes when the pain eases. The doctor told me how much of this to give y'."

"Malachi, I honestly think I would be dead this night if not for you."

"Begging y' pardon, Mr. Lee, but me-thinks God is taking care of y' more and better than I ever could. But I'll be right here through the night."

"That chaise should suffice for a nap, Malachi. Pull it close to the bed, and get a light blanket and pillow from the closet. The open window feels good with the breeze off The Central Park. I'm sorry for not being able to host you properly on your first visit to Mr. Oscar Alexander's home..." And just so quickly, Lee began to shake and flail about. "Malachi, I'm freezing cold. Please don't leave me ..."

Malachi took the blanket from his own chair and spread it tightly across the trembling frame of his friend. He got another one from the closet and laid it on. Obviously Mr. Lee's fever was rising. He slurred his words and when he finally stopped shaking, he stopped trying to talk and fell into a deep sleep, leaving Malachi alone with his thoughts.

The boy was far and away from anything he had ever known, albeit he knew what it was like to endure a long cold night on the fire escapes of the East Side Tenements. It was last winter that Malachi was as sick as a boy could ever be; his mother had just died; and he was an orphan without a home, without a soul on earth. He cried that night and a kind German woman rescued him from the fire escape, pulled him into her apartment, covered him with a ragged blanket, and there on the floor he spent the night. He guessed maybe two nights, as he was too sick to know.

He scanned the lovely room—the high ceilings, tapestry drapes outlining massive panes that were open half-way with gauzy white sheer curtains blowing in the summer-night's breeze on the Upper East Side of the beautiful City. He was in awe, never having seen such. Surely he was at *the king's table*.

Malachi stepped to the windows and closed them. It was warm in the house now. Mr. Lee should be okay. He didn't like seeing him flailing about with fever. Sleep was what he needed and time to let the shots work together with the laudanum to begin the healing.

Beyond the grandeur of the place, Malachi felt pity for Mr. Lee and the pain he was suffering at the hands of a madman who had broken all the rules of boxing.

He gave the barbarian a blimey good fight, thought Malachi, but I'll make sure he never again fights a man known for tearing the flesh of another with his teeth. But only one fight left, thank God.

Dawn broke over Upper Manhattan. Lee had slept soundly since the last dose of laudanum at half past three. He was still asleep. The room was hot, now, and Malachi thought it best to open the windows again. Warblers in The Central Park rendered a far more lilting tune than pigeons on the windowsills of the East Side tenements or the streets of the Bowery.

Malachi slipped to the bathing room, trying not to disturb Mr. Lee. There was time for him to sleep a little longer before he had to leave for work. They would be expecting him at the newspaper. How he would handle that Malachi would leave to him. The boy sufficiently cleaned the beautiful claw-foot tub and draped the two towels properly across the side to dry out. He wanted no blood spots anywhere.

He splashed his face with cold water and ran to the kitchen, in amazement gazing about. He had never seen such luxury. He opened the electric ice box to milk and butter and eggs, but how to prepare them escaped him. He ran a glass of cold water at the sink and drank it down then slipped back down the hall.

"Y' eyes are open, Mr. Lee. Do I dare ask how y' feel?"

"Amazing, Malachi. Maybe it is temporary, but between what the doctor gave me and your exceptional care during the night, I feel splendid."

"We'll see for real when y' try to sit on the side of the bed. I'll give y' a hand."

Lee, with pressure on his good side, attempted to stand.

"Take it easy for y're still effected by the laudanum. Sit there a minute and get y' bearings. Can y' have a glass of milk whilest y' sit?"

"That should work to give me some energy. Bring yourself one, as well, and we'll drink together, wishing we were at Hannigan's."

Malachi laughed, glad to see Mr. Lee with a little humor. He returned with the cold glasses and made sure Lee was comfortable holding his.

"Malachi, I've got to get to the paper this morning. They're expecting me. None of them know who in this world you are—yet. But can you go with me? It could be awkward, trying to explain you to them. I'm going to lean hard on you today until I can finish at the paper. I know I need a few days to recover before things can get back to normal."

"I'll do anything y' want me to, Mr. Lee."

"Charlotte will arrive in a couple of weeks, and I'm not ready to tell her about the fights. Maybe by then my wounds will have healed. So let's plan that last fight after she goes back to Lexington."

"That's a good plan, Mr. Lee."

"Where's your bicycle?"

"Chained behind Hannigan's."

"That's good to hear. Want to help me try to stand?"

"Yes sir."

Lee struggled to get his footing. He was sure it was the medication. He walked about the room with Malachi's help until he felt the blood flowing and his strength returning.

"Do you want to try and make ready the rig, or would you prefer to hail us a carriage ride to the newspaper?"

"I think 'twould be best to hail a ride. The walk down three flights of stairs will be hard enough and I'll need to help y' in and out. I think y' need to walk around a bit more to get some strength back before y' try the stairs."

"Then that's what we'll do. Look in the top drawer, the skinny one. On the right side is my money. On the left is yours in a long wooden box, if you want to count it. It will make you happy. Take some coins out of my side for the carriage fare and a couple of dollar bills in case we get hungry today."

Malachi grinned and said, "I don't want to count m' money yet. It will be a grand surprise one day. In fact, I have some to add to it from Hannigan's."

Lee nodded and smiled at Malachi's self-control.

"We must eat breakfast now. Some scrambled eggs and crusty bread buttered and warmed in the oven. Then we'll smear a lot of jam on. Does that sound good to you?"

"Yes sir," said Malachi, almost starving. Neither of them had eaten since earlier the day before.

"What do I do?" he said, getting the eggs and butter from the refrigerator. "I've never seen the likes of this kitchen. M' mother never had anything but an ice box. But then, we had little to nothing in it, anyway. We both wer' but skin and bones when she died."

"That's how I grew up, too, son. And that's what my folks have to this day. The South is far behind New York City in every way. We are blessed to be in the midst of plenty here. And I never had white bread until my grandmother came to New York. My mother, Cassie, makes hot flakey dark brown biscuits every morning. Dark brown, because that's what I always asked for."

He walked Malachi through the art of scrambling eggs in a bit of butter in a skillet on a gas burning cook stove. Malachi pondered how it must be in the southern hill town of Sarepta, Mississippi.

"We always have butter and milk in the ice box, because we have a milk cow. Almost everything we eat in the South comes from a garden that we work with our hands and a mule pulling a plow. Actually, as I look back, it's amazing. I miss that part of my life."

They ate sumptuously, spreading strawberry jam on the bread hot out of the oven.

"This is a bit of heaven," said Malachi. "But I wish someday to go to Sarepta in Mississippi and see y'r way of life. I would like to eat a dark brown buttered biscuit."

"With homemade blackberry jam—?"

Malachi smiled and licked the strawberry jam from his lips.

The weeks flew by. Lee had saved every penny he made at the newspaper and a drawer full of money from the three fights he had won. He would have more after Charlotte's visit, but only from one more fight. At least he hoped he would win so he could stop the absurdity. He had decided he would continue to fight until he won just one more. Then, he would concentrate on another idea he had. He was pondering writing for *The Elite Press*. He could do it in the afternoons after work and it should give him some extra money until he could start his job after the first of the year. Also, it was not an insane idea as was the bare knuckle fighting. And … his grandmother and Charlotte would love it, for he would write about the after effects of the war and the sensibilities of the Confederate generals. He never wanted to forget what they did for the South, the Confederacy. He would always be a Confederate, for he was what the Country referred to as a Real Son, a direct male descendant of one who died honorably in service for the South.

He would tell Charlotte about Malachi, but he had no plans to see him while she was in the City. He wanted to get her reactions to the young man once dubbed as a street urchin just from a conversation with her. He would know her feelings. He had spent a lot of time in deep thought concerning the situation. How could he expect Charlotte to have the same—could he say—parental feelings for Malachi O'Malley as he did, unless she knew something about him.

Chapter 12

Betrayed

It was early September when the Pullman thundered into the railway yard. Lee could see it from a distance, certain it would be Charlotte's. It slowed and coasted into the covered station at Grand Central. He stood on the cement platform, nervous and excited, looking from one car to the next, wanting to get first glimpse when she came into view. It had been months since he had seen her.

And there she was, stepping from the car, clutching her handbag and wearing a wide brim tightly-woven straw hat in the style of the models that graced the paintings of Oscar-Claude Monet, in just the hint of a daffodil, a rising sun—*soleil levant.* He wondered where she got these incredible hats. The yellow dress clung elegantly to her youthful body and begged a last few days of summer. He ran to her, took the articles from her hands and set them on the closest bench, drew her into his arms and kissed her so long and hard, for some strange reason thinking that, shortly, he may never see her again. Why had he felt so pensive? Sure, it had been a long time, but he had an unexpected sensation that left him with a disturbing uncertainty. Not at all the feeling of a rising sun, but a waning moon that slowly loses all hope of light.

"You look stunning, Charlotte."

"And you're as handsome as ever, Lee Payne."

"I've missed you so much. I'm sorry if it seems that I'm attacking you. I don't mean to, but quite frankly I didn't expect to over-react as I did."

"I quite liked your reaction, Lee, so don't apologize. I feel the same way. It has been far too long, and I, too, have missed you. I have had to practically chain myself to Lexington to keep from running away to New York City." She laughed, he closed his arms around her again, and pulling her head to his shoulder, he caressed her silky brown hair that had hung loosely below the hat.

"Let's get your baggage off the train," he whispered.

"I just brought one bag. I traveled with as little as possible, for it will only be a few days. And I'm thinking that maybe I will be returning home with a very large box."

"You will, indeed," said Lee. "And we will start that shopping excursion tomorrow."

He put the bag and her personal items inside the carriage and said, "Would you ride with me, ma'am? The sights are beautiful along the avenues, and you don't want to miss a thing. It's a great time of year in New York City with the trees starting to turn, and in this amazing yellow dress, you'll fit right in."

"I would love to ride with you."

He helped her to the driver's bench and said, "We will get you to Gilsey House so you can settle in and rest awhile, then I'll come and get you for dinner."

"By then I'll be ready."

"Well, you are very thin. We must make it a point to work on that the next few days. How about Delmonico's tonight and we can start the street wagons later? How does that sound?"

"Absolutely wonderful. I want some of all of it, especially from the pie wagon."

Lee wrapped his arms around her thin frame. "You need me, Charlotte, to take care of you."

"Yes," she said. "Our wedding day will be a glorious event, even if it lasts but ten minutes. I have dreamed of the day."

"Tonight we will set a date," he said.

Charlotte beamed, her smile lighting his heart.

They took the beautiful ornate halls and stairs to the third floor corner room facing Broadway. It would be Charlotte's first stay at Gilsey, and Lee had reserved his Grandmother Rachel's lovely old suite. He had only stayed at Gilsey once, himself. It was Christmastime when the family came to New York, surprising Rachel, arranged by Mr. Alexander long before he and his grandmother were married. Lee was younger than Malachi at the time and it was one of the most memorable times of his life.

Now, thinking about the fact that he had gotten so deep into a parental relationship with the lad without sharing his feelings with Charlotte worried him. He pondered his still-youthful way of doing things, hoping he would always be learning from his experiences and likely mistakes. He could not see himself handling this situation any other way. It was not only the righteous thing to do, it was humanitarian. He only hoped Charlotte would agree with him. He didn't want to put her on the spot, and he must give her ample time to make her own decisions which were becoming mandatory as far as Lee was concerned.

He helped Charlotte to her room and returned to *The Elite Press* to finish out his day as Carlisle was arriving for the evening shift.

"I'll bring Charlotte here on Monday, Carlisle. She will only be here for three days, and of course, she wants to see you."

"I will be happy to see her, too. I know it is a short visit, but soon we will have her with us for good."

"Yes," said Lee pensively.

"You seem a bit reluctant."

"Oh, no, it's not that at all. I just have a lot on my mind. Time and circumstance are causing my head to spin, but there are some things I need to discuss with you, Carlisle. Maybe we can do that after Charlotte leaves early next week."

"Well, you've peaked my interest."

"Do you remember when I brought young Malachi O'Malley with me to work a couple of weeks ago?"

"Yes, I do. A very nice lad."

"He's amazing, Carlisle. He reminds me of you and your relationship to Mr. Alexander. His story is much like yours."

"I can understand that, Lee. Are you saying you've become emotionally attached to him?"

"It's a long story, one that deserves time to tell. So, in the interest of that, I'll save the whole story until later. Soon, but after Charlotte leaves. I have to tell her that story tonight, and I'm now worried about how she will react. It's very important to me, but I don't think anything should be as important to me as the woman I plan to marry."

"You're absolutely right about that, Brother," said Carlisle. "Just take it slow and easy as you make your explanation. I'm sure the lovely Charlotte will be understanding, although I don't know to what degree you have attached yourself to the young urchin."

"That's just it, Carlisle. He has become like a son to me. I'm not sure why it all happened as it did, but Malachi has no one on this green earth besides me."

"That is poignant, indeed."

"Yes. I'll tell you more soon. Bring a handkerchief."

"Oh, don't do that to me, Lee."

"I have to, Brother."

It was early yet, the sun still high in the September sky, and sitting in the crescent booth at Delmonico's, Lee and Charlotte shared the moments while they waited for their server.

"I love this place, Lee."

"So do I, Charlotte. It has become the place of choice for the Payne family, I believe. Speaking of which, it won't be long now before you will be a part of the family. Are you ready for such?"

"It has dominated my thoughts for months now and, yes, I'm more than ready."

The waiter hovered with hot plates of steak and potatoes.

"I hope I'm not drooling," said Charlotte. "The aroma is delightful. I've never had an experience like this. I could be spoiled, Lee."

"Me, too."

They ate for an hour, savoring every morsel and talking nonstop, mostly about their hope-filled life together and working out a few details.

"I was thinking about January, shortly after New Year's Day. I know it will be cold, possibly even snowing. Would that bother you, Charlotte?"

"I would love that. A carpet of white with the red berry holly trees as decoration."

"Maybe Bow Bridge in the Central Park. Did I ever take you there?"

"No, but I would love to see it."

"It's made of cast iron, truly bowed and its color is as creamy fresh butter. In fact, in the winter it blends with the ice on the trees, sparkling in the sun. No cement on the floor of that bridge. It's all wood planks hand chosen from South America. I saw a wedding there from a distance one day. That gave me the idea. It's beautiful, especially now with the leaves falling. It's set in the trees, and it seems fitting that we get married on a bridge, though in no way is it like the bridge to Brooklyn. We'll add it to our excursion tomorrow. I'll pick you up at Gilsey about seven and we'll have breakfast at the Brownstone first. How does that sound?"

"Perfect," she said.

Lee whispered something to the waiter. "And two spoons," he said.

Charlotte smiled. Another one of Lee's surprises, and it delighted her to see the waiter return with one bowl and two spoons.

"Bread pudding!"

"I thought we would share. It's a large serving."

Charlotte dipped her spoon into the delicious treat that was smothered with orange sauce.

"Heavenly," she sighed, "Like this evening, which has been perfect. I'm filled with emotions, so happy to be with the man I adore."

Lee, reluctant to speak about Malachi, especially after what Charlotte had just said, paused in the conversation, not wanting to dampen the moment. But he had it to do. It was now or never. He conjured the courage and began to speak.

"Charlotte, I have something to tell you, and I have no idea how you will respond, so I guess I'll just spring and tell you and possibly suffer the consequences."

"Well, that sounds a little ominous. Should I worry?"

"No, at least I hope not. I wanted to tell you before we set the exact date for our wedding. I need to know how you will take this big announcement."

"Please tell me, Lee. You're scaring me."

He leaned toward her and began to tell his wife-to-be the story of the orphan boy, Malachi O'Malley, Charlotte wiping tears as he spoke. The easy part was painting the picture as he knew it.

"Now, how do I say this, Charlotte?"

Of course, this would be the hard part, for it could well impinge on Charlotte. He had no way of knowing until now. He must continue with this hitherto one-sided conversation.

"I've become emotionally attached to Malachi O'Malley. So much so that I feel a responsibility for him. But I would never do anything without your thoughts and reactions, and hopefully your consent."

Charlotte had never been one to entertain pent-up anger. Her gentle nature had always identified her, but now she sat mindless in the aftermath of the most beautiful, the saddest story ever. It was not in her character to do so, or she would have sent a glass crashing against the brick fireplace.

My consent to what?

In anger she fought tears, but no sound came from her lips. In fact, she was angrier than she had ever been in her life. He had betrayed her, and sadly she admitted to herself the extent of her jealousy and hurt. She sat still with tears popping from her eyes. And suddenly she was alone and pitiable, crying now not for the orphan boy, but for herself. Her eyes never left Lee's as she jerked her hand from his, picked up her bag, turned and hastened from his presence. Out the door and onto the crowded street she ran, hoping never to see him again, and she could hardly wait to get back to Gilsey House, pack her belongings and leave New York.

Lee was horrified, never expecting her to react in this fashion, much less to run. He clinched his fists, pondering what she had done and how he should respond. He shook like a leaf and fought to corral his emotions with no success.

Without control, tears filled his burning eyes and he took out his handkerchief. He thought about the day the dirty street urchin clumsily rumbled into the tenement neighborhood on his Boneshaker bicycle that looked more like a Civil War cannon than a two-wheeled ride. *M' name's Malachi O'Malley, pronounced Malachee—not the Jewish name. I'm Irish. Not Jewish.* And it was then and there a friendship commenced that should have lasted a lifetime. But she had ruthlessly snatched that from him. Had he given up both Charlotte and Malachi in this moment by trying to explain this matter of the heart?

He wondered where on earth Charlotte had gone. The big city was capable of swallowing one who knew little of its often contemptible tentacles. Now he realized what happened earlier at the train station. He was not only greeting the woman he loved, but he was saying goodbye at the same time.

She never said a word, thought Lee. What must she be feeling? Am I that insensitive to let this happen? And just who is going to be the one hurt the most in all of this? Lord, I have done a horrible thing. I spent all those weeks in agony, trying to raise enough money to marry Charlotte, all the pent-up warring emotions of the bare knuckle fight; all that I've done has been in vain.

The more he hashed over the circumstances, the more he knew—the Lord was righteously rebuking him for the fighting. Instead of rebellion, he bowed his head and received the admonition.

I will never again fight. How can You bless and lead me and fulfill my needs and desires if I cannot acknowledge Your rebuke? Help me, Lord!

Charlotte walked the streets of Mid-town Manhattan, afraid, lonely, and drawing a blank. Lee had just told her some street urchin had taken her place in his life. She walked vigorously down Fifth Avenue, across to

Broadway and finally to Gilsey House. She took the elevator to the third floor, her feet aching, burning from the long walk. She took a moment to soak them in the beautiful claw-foot tub and then searched for some socks in her bag. She slipped on her ugly, but comfortable, shoes, but at this point the ugliness of her shoes mattered not. Her dress would cover them anyway.

Lee, still sitting at Delmonico's, attempted to summon a plan, but his heart was not in it. His life had been plain and simple and then there was Malachi. Everything he had ever known suddenly had become complex. He had to do the right thing. He must be willing to give him up, say goodbye for Charlotte's sake, that is, if she would even take him back. But that would devastate Malachi. Being rejected could send him spiraling back to the filthy streets of Lower Manhattan. *I need thee, O, I need thee.* He cried, the old song his grandmother taught him to play on the violin ringing in his ears, and now the haunting tune and words gave him a measure of hope that God would arrest this turmoil and turn him in another direction.

Charlotte walked across the street from Gilsey to the park and sat on a bench. The tiny yellow leaves on the gingko trees fell like rain about the beautiful dress of the same color.

Why did I come? I've waited all these years to marry Lee Payne, not really knowing why it is taking so long for him to make up his mind. Now I know. Nothing ever works out for me. My papa died with Stonewall Jackson in that useless war. I'm fatherless and now this—this Malachi dilemma.

It was pitiful, painful. Charlotte was pitiful. And in her heart, she knew it.

What's wrong with me? Lee is also fatherless, yet he has seen fit to love me and a street urchin who is an orphan. Malachi has no father or mother. How utterly selfish of me. I'm so ashamed.

As quickly as she had entered into such self-centered thoughts, just so quickly she burst into tears again, crying aloud, begging God to forgive the selfishness and to give her a new heart toward Lee, one that would include Malachi O'Malley.

She ran to the street, hailed a carriage and stepped aboard after calling her destination.

"YMCA, McBurney, please."

Acknowledging the urgency in her voice, in minutes the driver was pulling in front of the brick building.

"Please wait," she shouted. At the desk, she inquired about Malachi. The attendant, an elderly man dressed in black, turned toward the mail cubbies then shuffled back to the desk with a note.

"Malachi has checked out for the evening. He works at Hannigan's in the Bowery until nine o'clock, at which time he should return. Is there a message for him?"

"No, no sir. No message for Malachi."

Charlotte ran back to her patiently waiting driver and shouted, "Hannigan's Pub in the Bowery, please."

The driver rolled his eyes, but clopped right along to the triangle, thinking, *Lady, you'll never get in that place.*

Charlotte was thinking the same thing. *I cannot get into Hannigan's. Women are not allowed in most pubs. Now what?*

Suddenly she was stuck in the world of man versus woman. She had never allowed herself to be any sort of women's rights advocate. And she was not about to start now. She was perfectly satisfied to live her life the way her mother had lived hers. Southern women loved their men and were devoted to them in all things. She had just made a terrible mistake, running out on Lee without a word. He may never forgive her, and she wouldn't blame him.

She begged the driver to stop on the side street to Hannigan's and wait at least ten minutes. The last remnants of day were fast fading, and in the light of the street lamp, she kept her eyes on the side door of the pub hoping, praying to get a glimpse of this boy. She tugged nervously at her hands, waiting for someone she didn't know.

And then—there he was. It must be him. A street urchin appeared in the first light of a crescent moon rising. She could see that he was tall and lanky, a handsome boy, wearing an Irish cap with auburn curls tight around his neck. Charlotte stepped down from the cabin of the carriage.

That's him, she cried. He's a beautiful boy. So kind looking. He has no one in the world besides Lee Payne. I love him, Lord. I want him, too!

She took a couple of steps toward the lad and began to cry out to him.

"Malachi! Malachi O'Malley!"

He stopped and searched for the voice that was calling his name.

"Here, Malachi! I'm Charlotte Elliott, Lee's friend."

Malachi looked perplexed at why Miss Charlotte would be in the Bowery, looking for him. He waved and when she waved both arms, he ran toward her.

"Miss Charlotte! What are y' doing here? Begging y'r pardon, ma'am. 'Tis glad I am to see y' for the first time in m' life, but where is Mr. Lee."

"Oh, dear Malachi," she cried adoring his Irish accent. "It's a long story. Have you finished your day?"

"No ma'am, but I can leave anytime."

"May I wait in the carriage for you?"

"Yes, ma'am. I allow 'twill be about five minutes. I have to wash m'self and change m' clothes."

"Where's your bicycle?"

Malachi grinned, delighted she knew about the bicycle.

"Behind Hannigan's."

"Bring it."

"Yes, Miss Charlotte."

The carriage driver affixed the red bicycle with rubber wheels to the back of the carriage and drove at a steady clip up Fifth Avenue toward The Central Park with Charlotte chattering the whole while, trying to explain to Malachi how circumstances had led her to him. Her point was not clear to him, though the urgency in her voice was.

"The moment I saw you, I was convinced that I would have done the same thing Lee Payne did when he first met you in the Bowery. I'm so sorry. I couldn't get that when he told me the story tonight. Sometimes seeing is believing."

Obviously, Malachi didn't know to what extent she was explaining herself. He would wait for Mr. Lee to straighten it all out. It sounded to him like Lee had plans to make Malachi a part of his family, which could mean Miss Charlotte would be an instant mother on her wedding day. If that were the case, Malachi knew it had caused something like a bare-knuckle battle between the two, one that neither could win without some fierce blows to the heart and soul. And Miss Charlotte had run away. He could not blame her, taking on full responsibility for a hurting, homeless human being, once a street urchin, was a lot to swallow in one gulp.

On the other hand, Charlotte had begun to think about having a fifteen-year-old son at her marriage to Lee. What could possibly be better than such an honor? She thought of her own loss and Lee's. It was hard enough living with one parent, but having no one—

The driver stopped at the Alexander Brownstone and they got out. He lifted Malachi's bicycle to the street. Charlotte soon learned that her insensitivities had cost her half a day's pay, but money well spent in her opinion. At least she hoped so. She added a nice gratuity and she and Malachi raced to the third floor to find the door locked. They waited on the cement steps at the ground floor, talking non-stop, watching eagerly to see Lee as he turned his rig into the Central Park across the street—and Malachi falling in love with Lee's girl.

Lee walked briskly across the street toward the Brownstone. It was near midnight and someone was sitting on the steps. The crescent moon was high in the sky over the Upper East Side, and he could see now that it was—

"Wait here," he shouted at the beautiful woman in the yellow dress and the street urchin he loved dearly. He ran back to The Central Park and retrieved his rig.

"Hop aboard! Up here with me, you two!"

Charlotte in her yellow dress and Malachi in his knickers and fine Irish cap rode on the driver's bench with Lee. The red bicycle rested firmly at the rear of the rig.

"What an amazing gift," shouted Lee Payne to the top of his voice.

They drove to Lower Manhattan, and in the brilliance of a million stars in a black sky above, and the city lights below, they sat on a park bench at the Battery, chattering, their arms around each other, Charlotte sitting between her two men.

"Lee, I have to keep saying how sorry I am. I was angry—bitterly angry— and hurting, and as it turns out, for such stupid, selfish reasons. I have never felt more comforted as in this moment. Forgiven and happy, sitting right here in this special place in the shadow of the Custom House and in the lamplight of Lady Liberty who welcomed our Malachi home to America."

Lee marveled that as he said goodbye to the fight—God filled His life with His wonderful presence and graced it with the two he loved the most—Charlotte and Malachi. How could he thank Him enough?

Chapter 13

As Love Would Have It—

Three days later, with gown purchased, all City excursions behind them, including hot apple pies from the wagons, plans made for a snow wedding on Bow Bridge in the Central Park, and strong ties binding the three together, Lee and Malachi drove Charlotte to the Grand Central Station. The three of them had filled every moment of her visit with as much joy as they could muster. Lee was still overwhelmed by feelings of thankfulness for the way things had worked out, when on that first night of Charlotte's arrival, he would not have given two cents for the possibility of ever marrying this girl he adored. Now he and Malachi were helping her aboard the Pullman that would take her back to her home in Lexington, Virginia. She would return to them shortly after New Year's.

"I've never taken the train before, Miss Charlotte, but I think I could enjoy that one day."

"You will love it, Malachi. Every boy should have a train ride about which to reminisce. There is a thrill in the experience that is past explaining. You'll see."

She stepped aboard, followed by Malachi who carried her wedding dress securely fastened in its box. Lee stepped up behind them with Charlotte's bag.

"I'll just say goodbye from here," said Malachi, after placing the box on the shelf in Charlotte's sleeping car. He hugged the beautiful lady that would soon be his acting mother, and turned to go. He looked back to see Charlotte wiping the tears from her face. And he hurried off the train.

"Lee, he's such a sweet boy. Are you positive we can have him?"

"No, not yet, but if it is perfectly fine with you, I will pursue it with the immigration authorities in the next few days. I think the way it all happened and the fact that I would not stop at the Custom House until we uncovered Malachi's citizenship papers and all we needed to know to prove his identity, I think our Miss Benoît will represent us to the authorities. I will keep you informed, and if they will let us adopt him, we will have to wait until you return and we're married so you can sign the papers with me. He's only three years away from age eighteen. Most young men are out and on their own before then. I'll say, Malachi has already put in his time of being alone in this world."

Charlotte nodded in agreement, finding it hard to speak.

"Listen to me, Charlotte. You don't know how happy you've made me. I know it was difficult for you to get used to the idea. It all happened quickly, but I know deep within, it is the right thing to do."

"I am sure of that, too, Lee. Don't think for one minute that I will change my mind about it. My moment of tantrum and self-centeredness is past. I have confessed and am forgiven, and I can assure you it will not happen again."

"And I want to reassure you, that you are not to blame for any of that, dear Charlotte. I didn't know exactly how to handle it and it was not my finest hour, that's for sure."

They laughed and held to each other for the moment they had left. Malachi waited on the cement platform with his back turned until Lee touched him, and they both waved until the train was out of sight.

The days and weeks passed quickly. September gave way to the howling winds of October, the leaves blowing to cover the City in yellow, orange, and brown. Lee Payne's shoulder had improved greatly, but he could see that the scar would always be with him. He dealt with the thoughts as best he could and sought to fill his days with better things. In fact, the more he thought about it, the more he realized that his relationship with Malachi would not have gotten as far as it did unless … unless he had been so determined to try the bare knuckle boxing. And … he had the scar to prove it. He had pressed for a companionship with Malachi, perhaps for the wrong reason at first, but as the relationship grew to that of a father and son, he could appropriate the adage "anything worth having is worth fighting for" and that included Charlotte and Malachi.

Lee had written his grandmother and Oscar Alexander revealing his thoughts and hopes of writing for *The Elite Press*. In fact, Oscar was elated and answered with enthusiasm. The more Lee pondered the desire to write, the more amazing reminiscences of the war from a *real* son's perspective filled his thoughts. Granted, he was a babe in his mother's arms when his father died, but he had seen the aftermath in the years that followed.

> Dear Lee,
>
> 'Twas with pleasure that I received your letter revealing your desire to write for *The Elite Press*. I have no doubt that you will be an extraordinary journalist, if you are anything like your grandmother, Rachel. Do not think I will hold it over you to be every bit as good as she, but I would love to read a draft of your idea for a first publication. We will go from there, if that suits you. And we will talk about paying you for your work. I hope you will consider writing for the newspaper even after you take on your new profession after the New Year. Writing will be an exciting addition to your calling. Do I dare hope and pray that you will write concerning the war years, the aftermath, and the years that have

followed? There is still so much to know and read and learn about those wretched days that eventually drove your grandmother to my side.

We look forward to returning to the City in time for your wedding to dear Charlotte. We're not sure, yet, how many of the family will be with us.

Let me add this … I want you and Charlotte to have Dixie and the carriage as a small gift of appreciation for your extraordinary care for the horse and carriage. I know you will always make sure your grandmother and I, as we grow older, will have a ride.

Until we see you again,
Oscar Alexander
October's End

Lee could not have known how Oscar Alexander would respond. It was a grand feeling to have his full approval. And the gift of Dixie and the carriage—well, he never in a million years would have expected that. There was yet a fearful thought—his family knew nothing about Malachi O'Malley.

Chapter 14

To Validate the South—

November brought an unexpected cold spell to Manhattan. Lee thought it expedient to find an apartment for his little family this week, if possible before snow started to fall. But first he wanted to comply with Oscar's request to read his first article for the newspaper.

He sat comfortably in the familiar space always occupied by his grandmother, Rachel, when she and Oscar Alexander were in the City. It was a beautiful office, more like a grand keeping room, entirely suitable for Rachel, with her feminine touches. He guessed it would always remain the same, for she was the center of life for Oscar, and he had carefully chosen the furnishings from his amazing stash of beautiful old pieces in the lower basement of the newspaper building.

Lee drew back the heavy brocaded window coverings and fastened the sides revealing an ample stream of sunlight and a grand view of Broadway traffic. The raised design of copper metallic threads cast a golden glow across the polished wood floors. Royalty, he thought. The place displayed beauty far greater than anything he had ever seen. He stepped to the wide paned windows and viewed traffic going and coming, surreys and fancy colorful carriages driven by shiny-faced black men in white finery. He stared for a few moments and marveled at the contrast—a far cry from the weather-beaten Old South buckboard pulled by a mule and driven by a shabbily-dressed boy of fourteen. He remembered the days and would take nothing for his heritage. He had seen and experienced both sides of life. Could he ever go back to the way it used to be?

Lee picked up his pen and began to write. The words spilled from his thoughts and his heart as fast as he could dip the pen in ink, and he scratched them upon the page. It was easy to write here, but 'twas from a biased point of view that Lee Payne began his story. He had nothing else to offer, for he was southern to the core. He would give it to Oscar unabridged and let him make the decision as to whether he would allow it to go to print at *The Elite Press*. Oscar would know what to do.

> My father, Albert Henry Payne, died in the Peach Orchard at Gettysburg. Likely as not, whether you hail from the North or the South, many of you lost the dearest on earth on that same Pennsylvania killing field. Truthfully, whether or not I deem it a useless and piteous war is not in question. Without a doubt that is the truth. The more I uncover of the details, the more hopeful I become of a better understanding that will satisfy my own curiosity. At the same time, I hope it will help you as you struggle with the right or wrong of that War Between the States.

It was mid-afternoon, chilly, and the wind whispered through the trees, sparse of leaves now, and like a withered old man seeking refuge, they hovered close to the front of the newspaper building on Broadway. Lee loved the sound of the wind when it passed through the naked trees. It was eerie, compelling, and made for a great writing companion. The spindly limbs clicked and clacked against the windows tapping out familiar sounds, like the keys on the teleprinters across the hall in the newsroom.

He stoked the smoldering fire with four logs and tended it until the blaze licked at the walls of the fireplace. The warmth would penetrate the room for at least a couple of hours. He picked up his pen again, dipped it in the indelible ink of truth as he saw it, for that was all he knew to tell. If he tried it any other way, which he would not, not ever—the people would know, for the truth is never negotiable. It sets men free. Rachel had taught him that a lie contaminates and dilutes the ink. He continued writing with hopes of completing the first in a series of how he knew it as a *real son* of a Confederate Soldier who died for his beloved South. For that reason, Lee was advantaged. He returned to the beginning of his article and inserted a title that read, *They Who Inherited Courage.*

> Even now, not too many years before the turn of a new century, maybe the man who could articulate the grossness of the war years has not yet been born. I have no doubt that one day that man will appear on the scene, a man who has a backbone like a saw log and instead of merely describing victor and vanquished in terms of endearment, will tell the hard truth concerning the nemesis who was at the heart of the ruination of the South. I will gladly beg my grandmother to let that person read the letters my grandfather, my father and my uncles wrote home while it was all taking place, although they never invoked the name of Lincoln in their letters. I've often wondered why, but, at that point, they were mostly interested in protecting the family and farm they had left behind than laying blame on Lincoln or anyone else.
>
> I was born in 1862, not too many months after the Payne men, including my father, left our home in the hills and marched off on foot to join the Mississippi Volunteer Army of Ten Thousand. It remains hard for me to imagine the extent of the hardship they faced from the beginning. Calluses formed on their blistered feet

after weeks of marching across Mississippi, Tennessee, and up into Kentucky where they would take their artillery training in the cold winter snow. Onward they marched until they were favored by God and the rail cars to a ride that gave hours of rest to weary feet and legs, as they stretched their tired frames across the cold wood plank floors and slept to the blessed sounds of iron thundering against iron, the sounds of rain beating hard against a tin roof, their weary minds hoping the ride would never end. I allow they wished for just one quilt from Grandmother's quilt box as they shivered and clung to one another for warmth.

I have no personal knowledge of the times, only what I've been told by the Payne men who returned from the war, and from my grandmother, Rachel, who was the voice of Sarepta's women when their men were gone. And when they didn't come home, and those women and children needed someone upon whose shoulder to cry, she grieved with them, for she had given all.

I grew up in the aftermath while Mississippi reaped no rich rewards from Reconstruction. That war had devastated the Southland, pushed us back into the darkness, and left us with little hope that we would ever rise from the ashes. But—we did. That's when I knew firsthand the resilience, the steadfastness of southern people.

I took my basic training at age five and six on the banks of McGill Creek, swinging on grapevine and sliding down soapstone with my Uncle Samuel, who was just two years older than I. I knew every tree and bush by name. I could recognize most by the delicate fragrance of the blossoms. There's nothing like the privet bush, its heady scent reaching for miles. I loved it, but if you have an aversion to it, the privet can be hateful. You could be weeping when you were happy.

It was a cover up during the war years, for our people cried far more than they laughed. Like most barefoot boys, the earth's fragrances are locked in my memory and senses, which to this day, remind me that God has an amazing way of cheering us when, within ourselves, there is nothing to be cheery about.

But as a child, my days and nights were not filled with thoughts of the war and its aftermath as were the older folks. Those thoughts would come later for me. In fact, as the years passed and I grew up, I found myself destined to study what I call the Cruel War, for it was a far cry from civil. Four years at West Point Military Academy saturated me in the events from both sides, all theatres. In hindsight, of course.

I have thought much about how the seemingly untamed uprising of youthful Southerners took place in 1861, the year before I was born. They were standing up *for inherited convictions and constitutional rights as they understood them.* It might have been ill-defined to those outside of the South, but it was in grand harmony to the men who lived it. As clear as the sounds of Dixie strummed out on some old farmer's banjo and the drum and fife of the fourteen year old boy called to war for a purpose. And, once again, I visualize my family and their friends from Sarepta as they dropped their plows, tied their mules, and rushed to the front lines with squirrel rifles and double-barreled shotguns, to defend all they held dear. Liberty was at stake.

My heart swells with pride when I think of my grandfather, Thomas Goode Payne, my father, Albert Henry, and Uncle Jonathan who, after the war, became my father. And Uncle Isaac who joined the Army when he reached the age of seventeen, fought out the war and returned reasonably sane, just in time to endure Reconstruction and the aftermath and the

> insensibilities of the issues that were laid at the door of the South by the Carpetbaggers and Scalawags and Copperheads—an extension of the demons that were bent on enabling the men who were left in Lincoln's Radical Republican Regime. But men like my Uncle Isaac, and my step-father, Jonathan, and those we knew who came back with grit and determination—these are they who inherited courage, conviction, and a strong understanding of the Constitution. I shall, with determination, carry on the legacy.
>
> To be continued …

Lee Payne was exhausted from dredging thoughts of the past, thoughts that he had gleaned from his family through the years. Exhausted more from the memories of those early years—as he learned more about his father who died on the killing fields of Gettysburg—than he was from the day's work. Although he was not on duty, he checked in with the printers and poured himself a glass of cold water, then returned to Rachel's chair. He had not intended to write more than one article this evening, but he was not ready to stop. He followed his journalistic heart, for the time being, and continued, thinking of the ragged form of his father, Albert Henry—crawling out of the railroad cut and running as fast as his tired legs would take him until he dropped under the heavy fire of the Union Army—giving every ounce of his red blood for the South that day. And the next in the series, based on his knowledge, he entitled, *The Greatest Controversy.*

> My Grandmother Rachel faithfully sought to inform me as best she could for many years just what happened between 1860, the year that Mississippians made plans to secede from the Union, and 1870, the year the Union restored us. That plan was thwarted by Lincoln and a Radical Republican Regime that had other plans for the South. Great was the controversy, but Rachel assured me the South had not deserved to bear the blame of

sectional differences alone, that they had been willing to claim their borders and walk away peaceably according to the Constitution. The double-minded Lincoln had been determined to claim the South was in violation of the Constitution on March 4, 1861, when on January 12, 1848, he had declared in any state a people had that right. Rachel had cried many times telling me the story.

I am exceedingly proud to be a true Son of the South and the Confederacy, and I need no other to validate the South's role in the war and exactly why they felt it necessary to leave the Union in the first place. Rachel was careful to make sure I knew that I have nothing of which to be ashamed. When I was old enough, she let me read the letters from my Grandfather, Thomas Goode Payne, my father, Albert Henry, and my Uncle Jonathan. She wanted me to know the real reason they left it all to go to war, and not one letter mentioned slavery. My folks didn't own slaves. So … I guess that means if only one of those northern generals or their wives owned slaves, it was one more than my family owned. And I might say here that Gen. Robert E. Lee, for whom my father named me from the battlefield, set his slaves free before he went to war. The same cannot be said for Lincoln's finest general, nor for the majority of northern slave owners. I suppose Grant did not have the heart to rid himself or his wife of her beloved servant, Jule. I do not say that with malice, for I truly believe, from all I have read since the war, that Mrs. Grant loved her slave.

There were incidents where North met South in controversy at West Point long after the war, and I allow it will always be that way, but that is not what matters any more. In my years at the Academy, I conscientiously poured over strategies of the South's finest warrior generals. Their heroics were amazing. Of course, I am emotionally attached to the memory of Gen. Robert E. Lee, who has already gone down in American history as the greatest warrior-patriot to have ever lifted a sword for the South. And perhaps none was braver than Gen. John B. Gordon of Georgia, a brilliant southern general who fought and was wounded in more battles than one could count.

When the war was over, Union Gen. Grant unwaveringly determined to see that the South and its people were treated with fairness and dignity as the states made their voluntary re-entry into the Union, one by one, and Gordon had recognized that. This was a sensitive time in history. I was aware of the sensitivities from West Point, and many times I had to bite my tongue to keep from speaking controversially. It would not have been worth it to use my fists to even the score. Though I could have done it physically, I could never have effectively changed anything with violence and a bad attitude toward my northern brothers.

The greatest controversy and the greatest enigma to me was that if Lincoln was dead set on his argument that the Union had never been broken because the South had left unconstitutionally, why—just why were they mandated to raise their right hand again, re-pledge allegiance, pay their taxes, create a new State constitution and re-submit it to get back into a Union that Lincoln declared had never been broken in the first place? That does not make sense to me. In fact, it is foolish, like force-feeding a true southerner collard greens, sweet potatoes, and pickled pigs' feet when the love for such is second nature. But Lincoln was killed before he would ever have an opportunity to put his personal foot down. It got done for him by his Radical Regime. I cannot help but wish Lincoln had lived for many reasons—

To be continued …

Late in the afternoon, Lee stood and walked around briefly to get the circulation moving in his feet and legs. He thought how tiring it was to sit for long periods of time, writing, especially about something as controversial and heart-rending as the war had been. But when he thought of Albert Henry, he felt so rebuked, threw his head back and gasped as he visualized his father's struggle, thinking surely he could endure a few hours of writing and sobbing to tell his story. Not wanting to light another fire for the night, he retrieved a blanket from Rachel's closet, wrapped himself in it, sat down, and continued his series under the title, *A Final Salute.*

> An inherent compassion for humanity obviously guides me, as I do not wish death on any man, but I do wish Lincoln had lived for other reasons. He needed to have freed himself—to ask for forgiveness—not that he necessarily would have, but just maybe he would have asked to be forgiven for the lies he told concerning the South and its intentions for leaving the Union and desiring to just be left alone. But the world would never see Lincoln fall to his knees and beg forgiveness for the deaths of so many sons of the North and the South. For the remembrance of some trigger-happy, unnecessarily over-eager actor who took no time to consider the consequences of his actions, would hover like a dark cloud from that awful day to perpetuity. Lincoln had squandered his ample opportunity to beg forgiveness.
>
> Even the hated General Sherman had shown mercy on the South and its people at war's end—whether to salve his conscience for the inconceivable damage he had done and the vicious manner in which he had done it—and his compassion that day was interrupted by the Republican Regime. They felt he was allowing too much mercy toward the South, hence the extent of Sherman's leniency was disallowed by Gen. Grant. Can you imagine it, a merciful, lenient Gen. Sherman? The man

who, in a violent display of madness, marched across the Confederate state of Georgia to the Sea, wreaking havoc, killing the South's women and children, raping and burning the land. He was now attempting to show mercy?

It is at this point that I remind myself of just how uncivilized Major Gen. William T. Sherman was to say in a letter to one of his subordinates: "The Government of the United States has … any and all rights which they choose to enforce in war—to take their lives, their homes, their lands, their everything… war is simply power unrestrained by the Constitution … To the persistent secessionist, why, death is mercy, and the quicker he or she is disposed of the better …" Sherman was claiming the right to annihilate every secessionist. If the world thought this evil man was kidding, they may want to read this letter that is archived for posterity.

At least Grant had graciously refused to permit Union artillerymen from firing a celebration salute of victory over the surrendered Armies of the South that day at Appomattox. He knew—Grant knew the South had been humiliated enough. The war was over, so was the humiliation, at least as far as Gen. Grant was concerned.

I remember only what I've been told, but I do remember, first hand, the tale of Uncle Joab's journey to Gettysburg with a stop in Washington City, and the chance he took to see President Ulysses S. Grant in the Nation's White House. And now this soldier, warrior, president was gone, having died an early death in 1885 just twenty years after the close of the war.

I'm not sure my family feels the same way I do. Maybe Uncle Isaac does. He had been the one left at war's end, waiting at the white picket fence that surrounded Appomattox Court House and absorbing

> Grant's amazing actions as a United States military soldier, and not an enemy of the South that day. Isaac was privileged to see Confederate Gen. Gordon gallantly caught up in the historical moment and in his best pomp and ceremony, face Union Gen. Chamberlain. In his glorious soldier's posture and bearing, Gordon wheeled his horse, gently touching him with a spur, and as if one with his faithful ride, caused him to rear and bear and in fluid motion, his horse gracefully swung down and bowed while Gordon touched the point of his sword to the toe of his boot in a final salute of vanquished to victor. He spoke the words, sending orders back for his troops to follow protocol. And one by one they submissively laid down their arms and standards.
>
> To be continued …

Lee was determined to write the last article before he left for the evening. It was something he had to do, as though he were unction'd now and may never be again. He may have called it, *The Last Tattoo*, but it was more than that, for the boys had all struggled with the giving up of the standards that represented who they were and what they stood for. So this one he titled— *Hard Things of the Past.*

> I envision the faithful Gen. John B. Gordon and his warrior horse performing duty that day. When the sword touched the boot of the saddened Confederate officer, it had to have been the most humiliating of experiences. The vanquished had become footstool to the victor.
>
> They said, *Farewell, dear Southland and all that you might have been*, and they shed yet another tear as they dropped their standards in a pile, but not before pressing the remaining blood-stained threads to their lips and saying good-bye.

But not every Confederate soldier was at the Appomattox Court House that day. Most of them were still in the field, and they burned their regimental flags to keep them out of the hands of the Yankees. Some tore them into bits and pieces and handed them out, a sad remembrance of the Cruel War. Some in the field hid their flags and risked being captured in the days before the surrender at Appomattox.

So many *little foxes have spoiled the vine*, and I, once again, ponder secession, determined to know what on earth had provoked Lincoln to become so radical in his over-reaction to the South's decision to leave the Union. I have to include the insidious thought that he could never abide a legacy of southern secession that would have hailed his presidency a failure. But I do call to mind that thousands of men and boys were killed in action because of his decisions.

It was on Lincoln's watch that these men and boys died and that the South's brave men were buried together in mass trench graves all over the beloved Southland in soil that belonged to them.

It was on his watch and at his call that southern soil—a part of the United States of America according to Lincoln—was laid waste by a gratuitous and pathetic executive order.

And it was because of Lincoln's false mandate—that the Union had never been broken—that history combined the death counts to well over 620,000 men and boys. Over half of those were Union; the other half, Confederate soldiers.

It troubles me that the South is yet stuck in the muck of memory, for there will come yet another time when we will all be called on to fight for our country, the United States of America.

Wars have raged since the twenty-sixth century before Christ. Every Chinese Dynasty has either waged war or fought a war. Year after year after year. There will always be war in some corner of the earth, and either the United States will meddle in the affairs of other countries or we will legitimately go to the rescue when we are needed. The American government is obsessed with warring countries, maybe legitimately, maybe not. We each have our opinions, that is, unless something happens to throw us into a state where our opinions are silenced by a government as corrupt as the Radical Republican Regime. I have no penchant for politics, and I have had my fill of thoughts of war and carnage as it happened between the North and the South. The politics of Sherman and Grant and Lincoln were despicable and should never have been brought to the public arena. Our country, the United States of America, is better than that.

The Radicals only had heart for the North and for years the South had little help to clean up behind the havoc the North wreaked upon it. For years it looked doubtful that the South would ever again be equipped and ready for life, much less for war. But we *have* recovered, and whether or not it would have been to the best interest of North and South for the Confederacy to have remained a viable country—well, we may never know the answer to that question. For five years the South was a country with a flag and a constitution and eleven consenting sovereign states, and hope for a bright future, with no reason for not living, moving, and having our being as neighbors with the Country from which we seceded.

I have labored under the reminiscences of the war years, the hard things of the past, the things which might come in the future, and the things about which

> we can do nothing. There is much for us all to learn so that the deck will not always be stacked against the South. The half has not been told, but this southern boy will be found faithful to tell it as long as there is breath within me.

Lee was finished. He closed his thoughts, satisfied that he had properly and without malevolence exercised his First Amendment Right—adopted December, 1791, as one of the first ten amendments to the Constitution that make up the Bill of Rights—by voicing his personal opinion. He was reasonably sure that he would not be arrested as so many of his predecessors had been during the war years. Lincoln had many newspaper editors and journalists arrested and imprisoned for exercising their right to freedom of the press and free speech.

The fire had no spark left, and the room was cold, as was he. But it was time to leave and no one would be occupying Rachel's room, so he would not stoke another fire. The sun slowly inched toward the horizon.

He climbed the stairs to the attic of the old newspaper building and took the steps to the roof. He could view east or west from where he stood, the sunrise over the East River; sunset on the Hudson. There was nothing more beautiful to him than the mistiness of a cold November sky and a vanishing sun leaving thick layers of pink and blue to slowly disappear below the Manhattan skyline on New Jersey's shore, making room for the stars to fill up the skies and light the night.

The sun was gone for the day, but the lights of Manhattan and Brooklyn mysteriously encircled him. It was not so long ago that electricity had begun to brilliantly illuminate the avenues of New York City. Lee could ride in his carriage from the Windsor Hotel to the Cunard Wharf through four miles of brilliantly lit streets, glowing in the flicker and enchantment of the luminaries. He had been told that long after the Dutch first established a trading post on the Western Shore of Manhattan Island in 1613, and the British in 1697 claimed ownership, the Common Council mandated certain houses stay gas-lighted during the night so that the City would never completely fall asleep. There would always be light as the residents took measures to make it happen.

He had memories of the day the final span was completed on the Brooklyn Bridge, gaslights aglow during the night on both sides of the Gothic Arches and at daylight, the crowds rushed to walk it from Brooklyn to Manhattan for the first time. He was there, embracing the historic moments, waiting at the granite arches for Charlotte. That was the day he placed the ring upon her finger, a total surprise to her. And now these years later, the gaslights had been replaced with electric ones, and a lot of water had flowed under that bridge between two cities. These were exciting days.

At times Lee Payne experienced an unalterable attachment to Manhattan's British roots. But then, at other times, he knew his roots were deeply planted in the red clay hills of Mississippi, on McGill Creek, in Calhoun County. He had learned to do both effectively without betraying either.

Chapter 15

A Place to Call Home

Lee Payne had written the articles quickly, the words springing from his heart, not surprisingly, for he had harbored these reminiscences for many years. He arranged them in order, breaking at crucial intervals with the words, *to be continued*—and folding each to fit the envelope he had made from heavy brown paper, he was finished. He hoped they would meet Oscar Alexander's approval. They were his contribution to those who loved and appreciated the Confederacy for its true worth. He was intensely determined that the "Ancient Landmarks" of thought would never be quelled or squandered. For the most part, they were gleanings from personal experiences told in the war letters of his grandfather, his father, and his uncles. He had read them all. How proud he was of his forebears who fought for all the right reasons! No one could take that away from Lee Payne. He boarded his rig and steered Dixie toward the Post Office with its flying buttresses. He would mail the package of articles and wait to hear from Mr. Oscar.

Malachi climbed onto the end stool at Hannigan's, waiting for Lee to arrive. He had finished cleaning for the day, the floors scrubbed and the tables and bar polished. He had washed himself and changed his clothes, excited for this day. He would be going with Mr. Lee to search for an apartment on the rail line. It was mid-November and the wind blew fiercely on Lower Manhattan's East Side.

"There you are," shouted Lee as he entered the squeaking door at Hannigan's. "Where's your coat? It's freezing cold out there."

Malachi didn't want to say it, but he had to. "I don't own a coat, Mr. Lee."

Of course, Lee knew that.

"Well, you do now." He pulled a fine woolen Navy peacoat from the package in his hand. And behind it, a red scarf and a gray Irish apple cap.

"For me?"

"None other," said Lee, smiling.

"Tis a fine gift, Mr. Lee."

"You deserve it and more. Besides, I would rather buy coats than pay hospital bills, and how can I possibly wear this fine woolen coat Grandmother Rachel gave me while you are wearing a scanty shirt and knickers? And, too, I will expect you to wear this as you stand with me at the altar of Bow Bridge when I say my vows to Miss Charlotte Elliott."

"That, Mr. Lee, will be a privilege."

"And maybe we can think of a shorter name for you to call me on that day. I'll let you pick."

Lee smiled, knowing what he wanted that name to be.

"I found some apartments listed in *The Elite Press*. I thought we would try those first. I've never done this before, so I really don't know what to expect. I've brought along enough money from the drawer to pay for three months, starting December 1, and I believe it will be enough for that. God has been gracious to us, Malachi."

"I have money on the other side of that drawer to contribute, too, you know."

"No, Malachi, we likely will not need any of that side of the drawer, and I was hoping we could save that for—maybe West Point Military Academy. That is, if you continue to make excellent progress in your schooling. I think you probably have two more years after this one, and you will be ready to graduate schooling—with honors."

"West Point!"

"What would you think about that?"

"I would die for that, Mr. Lee."

"Well, keep it in mind as you pour over the harder subjects, son. You can do it, but when you get there, believe me, you will think you *are* dying."

They boarded the rig, which now belonged to Lee and Charlotte and Malachi, thanks to Oscar Alexander. All three of the apartments were in the same building.

"Do you prefer the ground floor or fourteenth, Malachi?"

"Oh, I could never choose, Mr. Lee."

"Well, let's just look at all three and maybe together we can make a good decision. It costs only a nickel to ride the rail, and although you will not be living at the YMCA, you will be going there for your classes, at least the rest of this year. We will see how far you can get on the rail and, then, some days you can ride your bicycle."

"Mr. Lee, I'm beginning to feel like a southern elitist. I know I'm not to get 'puffed up'—that's from scripture, the Apostle Paul said it. I know y' know what it means, but I didn't. I'm supposed to be humble, and I need to be reminded all the time, because good things keep coming m' way, and I don't ever want to take any of it for granted."

"I feel the same way, Malachi. Sometimes I think of my stepfather, Jonathan, and my mother, Cassie—they still have it hard. Southern life is not easy. It's all physical, tiring farm work, but when you are accustomed to it, well, it's not so bad."

"I can't wait to find out for m'self."

"Are you ready to go? Put your coat and things on, and it's okay to be proud. The only thing is we have to stop off at Mr. Stewart's Store and get you some long black trousers. You look downright funny with part of those long legs showing."

"Y' cannot make me feel bad, Mr. Lee. I'm too set on looking proper today."

Malachi whispered his excitement to Lee. "This place has an elevator?"

"Yes, and because of that we might want to take the apartment on the fourteenth floor, for the view, whatever that may be."

"Is it the top floor?"

"Yes."

"Then maybe there's an entrance to the roof."

"That will be important," said Lee.

For an hour, the two looked at the three places, one of which could be their home, at least for a few years, keeping Miss Charlotte in mind as they made their decision.

"Well, now that you've seen them all, what do you think, Malachi? Can we choose from these three?"

"Oh, I think so," said Malachi. "Of course, I love them all. The very thought of *home* makes m' happy. I like something about all three of them, but the fourteenth floor is m' choice for several reasons."

"Let's hear it."

"I like the height, the bigger windows across the front, the French doors to the balcony and the wood burning fireplace. And don't forget the furnishings are splendid, and the view from the roof is spectacular."

"Those are my very top reasons, too. And you'll have your own bedroom. The bathing room is sufficiently large enough, and I think Miss Charlotte will love the kitchen. Come to think about it, I hope she can cook, Malachi!"

"I won't tell her y' said that, Mr. Lee."

"We're in agreement. Let's go Malachi."

They took the stairs down fourteen flights to the front desk.

"We'll take the apartment on the fourteenth floor, ma'am."

Lee signed the papers, paid the money, and they left satisfied they had made the right decision.

"She said we can move in December 1. That will give us plenty of time to get ready for Miss Charlotte, Malachi."

"Can we do a bit of Christmas decorating? I know where we can get leftover evergreen branches. I see it every year on the streets of the Bowery. It smells so good."

"Yes, indeed, and we can have our real Christmas after the wedding so Miss Charlotte can be with us. Grandmother Rachel and Samuel taught me how to decorate for Christmas. We can get a lot of things in Central Park. Pine cones and boughs, sweet gum balls, and red holly berries."

"And 'twill smell good, that apartment of ours," said Malachi.

Part Two

The lonesome whistle of the Pullman and the
yellow light in a foggy day and
thoughts of his father in the mountains of
Kentucky resting on the cars
stirred his emotions, and under his feet he
could feel the rumble on the rails a mile away.
The little things make life better
for me, he thought.
I hope Papa felt the same way.

Chapter 16

The Greatest of Gifts—

Thanksgiving Eve, Lee Payne sat quietly in Rachel's chair at *The Elite Press*. He read the words over and over. His words. They belonged to him, and now they belonged to every reader who dared. His first article had gone to press on this day with Oscar's full approval. Lee was thankful for so many things. He reached for the Bible that lay permanently in its place on Rachel's desk, opened it to Psalm 34, seeking to be blessed this season by the reading of the thoughts of King David, who was a far greater writer than he. Rachel had taught him how to read the Psalms, gleaning every promise and thought from the Old Testament as it concerned Jesus, the Messiah. David had said, "I will bless the Lord at all times; his praise shall continually be in my mouth." He read it all, twenty-two verses.

He began to recall blessings of the past year, and as fast as he could keep ink on his pen, he filled up the white piece of paper in front of him.

When he got to Malachi, he dropped his pen, tears formed in his eyes and he shook. Lee could take no credit for rescuing the lad from the streets of New York City, from loneliness and hopelessness. From certain peril. The blessing was all his, but there was some unfinished business.

His day at the Press ended, and Lee wrapped the warm scarf about his neck and snatched his coat from the hook in the common hall. He waved good-bye as he passed the press room, and hurried out the big wooden front doors of the newspaper building. Climbing aboard his rig, Lee noticed he still had Rachel's Bible in his hand. *Good! He thought. But I will guard it with my life and promptly return it.*

It had been a few days since Lee had spoken to Malachi. He wondered if the boy ever doubted him. Somehow, he thought not. Their relationship was solid, as close as father and son. Of course, neither remembered their birth fathers as they both died when the boys were under two years of age. That gave them some common ground.

It took awhile for Lee to twist and turn through the Thanksgiving traffic. For some reason, people were always raucously rushing from one department store to another in the City. On the day before Thanksgiving, he allowed Macy's and Mr. Stewart's stores were fully packed with shoppers. He would not want to be inside either one, elbow to elbow and eye to eye with women aggressively vying for the item some other shopper was holding in her hand. He was not used to having a lot of worldly possessions and he could never become one with these people yet pledged to never be bothered if Charlotte chose to be one with the mad shoppers.

He arrived shortly after five o'clock as the sun was casting its last glorious rays across the New Jersey side. Lee stopped at the front desk and sent for Malachi, who bounded immediately down the steps to the lobby. When he saw Lee, his face lit up like the gas lights on Broadway.

"Mr. Lee, 'tis great y're here. It's the day before Thanksgiving and I wanted to see y' before then."

"And I had this urge to see you, too, son. I wanted to tell you I will pick you up in the carriage in the morning and we will search out a place to enjoy Thanksgiving Dinner, although I can tell you—I don't believe the turkey and festive foods will come close to what will be on Grandmother Rachel's table in Sarepta tomorrow."

"Maybe next year, Mr. Lee."

"I hope so, Malachi. Thanksgiving in the woods of Calhoun County cannot be explained. You have to experience it."

"I will cheer the day when I can find out for m'self."

"Can you ride with me to The Central Park for a couple of hours? We can hail a pie wagon for some deliciousness and find a park bench."

"Indeed," said Malachi, about to have a conniption. "That makes m' excited."

The two rode up Broadway toward The Central Park, Malachi much quieter than usual, his silence suddenly compelling. And then he spoke.

"Mr. Lee, I've been thinking about all the good things. So much has happened since I met y', so many good things. I know we've talked a lot about the important things. But I fear I'm putting the good things ahead of the most important thing in m' life."

Now, Lee knew where this conversation was going. He had waited for the day, wishing for Malachi to bring up the all-important talk they must have. And now it was time. He pulled the rig to a pleasant place in the Park and stopped near a canopy of scaly bark trees, their skinny limbs clanking against each other, for they had dropped the last of their leaves upon the ground in a blanket of brown, a monochromatic semblance of autumn. Soon the leaves would decompose and eventually receive their first covering of snow, another scene would unfold on the streets of New York, and they would celebrate yet another season. They sat on the park bench and Lee waited while Malachi finished his explanation and began to pour out his heart in confession.

"I know I'm only fifteen. I have been blessed to have the great preachers of Lower Manhattan share so much with m' in our Bible studies, and of course y', Mr. Lee, have shown m' the love of Christ and y've taught m' so much about Jesus. I know He is the Savior of the world and that a decision to have Him as m' own is personal. Well, I have come to the end of m' sinful self, and though I have not committed crimes, I know who I am—I need Jesus to go with m' to the ends of the earth and that means I have to do something."

Malachi's eyes filled with tears and Lee choked back his own. He was hearing Malachi's confession of faith.

"I want to have Christ as m' Savior now. Will y' help m', Mr. Lee?"

"Malachi, this pleasure will be mine, with all glory to our Heavenly Father for drawing you to Himself. You know, Jesus said those very words in John 6:44. 'No man can come to me, except the Father who hath sent me draw him: and I will raise him up at the last day'. That covers exactly what you just said—that you need someone 'to go with you to the ends of the earth'—all the way to heaven."

Lee took Malachi slowly and deliberately through the Scriptures so there would be no later questioning and wondering. Thankful he had memorized all those verses that Rachel had taught him through the years, Lee, with his hand firmly upon his grandmother's Bible, shared each of them with the lad.

"Malachi, do you believe all that I've told you which is clearly in the Scriptures?"

"Yes, Mr. Lee, I believe."

At that, Malachi dropped to his knees and laid his head on the wooden park bench. Lee knelt beside him.

"One more thing, Malachi, believing is almost getting you there, but there's something else Jesus wants you to do. You have clearly confessed that you are a sinner and in need of a Savior and that you believe in Jesus. Now this is a powerful verse from John chapter one. *But as many as received Him, to them gave He power to become the sons of God, even to them that believe on His name.*"

"I get it, Mr. Lee—I believe, now I must receive Jesus."

Still on his knees, Malachi called upon the Heavenly Father and received His Son, Jesus. Aloud, he cried out and prayed like Lee had never heard before. Tears were streaming down Lee's face as Malachi made his full confession of faith in Christ. Lee embraced Malachi and said, "Now, you are truly my brother, son. And life is just beginning for you, Malachi."

Lee remembered the white paper he had left on Rachel's desk. Under Malachi's name he would write yet another blessing of the year—*Malachi became my brother for real on this day and … "I will bless the Lord at all times; His praise shall continually be in my mouth."*

Chapter 17

The Good and the Bad—

Scarfing down a big piece of brown-paper-wrapped pumpkin pie, Malachi said, "This is the best pie wagon in New York City. And I don't think I've ever had this kind."

"We grow pumpkins in our gardens in Sarepta."

"Really? What is a pumpkin, anyway?"

Lee laughed and described a pumpkin as best he could. "You can't eat pumpkin without some added ingredients, such as eggs and butter, milk and sugar and spices like cinnamon and nutmeg."

"That really sounds good."

"That's what you're eating."

Malachi smiled and when he was finished, he gazed longingly at the pie wagon.

"Here," said Lee, tossing him a quarter. "Get two more slices. I feel the same way."

They finished the southern treat and sat on the park bench, hardly able to move. The sun was brilliant, the wind cold. A perfect combination.

"Tomorrow, we will go to Lower Manhattan and see if Fraunces Tavern is open and serving a Thanksgiving meal. I want you to know the history of that place back to the Revolutionary War and Gen. George Washington. You're going to be the most educated Irish immigrant in America, besides you'll have to know all of this when you get to West Point."

"I love that y' teach m' so much about this country," said Malachi.

"I want you to know it all—the good and the bad. And although I am definitely outspoken about my southern heritage, I never want you to think I'm forcing my political or religious views on you."

"Don't worry. I think I'm already a southerner by choice, Mr. Lee."

"Well then, let me share a few more things about which I am extremely passionate. You can draw your own conclusions, and remember Grandmother pretty much taught me everything I know about that War of Northern Aggression. Most of her information came from the newspapers at the North. They covered all of the war news. And she knew. She went to great lengths to search and research all these writings to gain her knowledge."

Malachi made himself comfortable on the wooden park bench, faced the sun and hoped it would not burn his fair skin. It felt too good to resist.

"First, I'm so proud of you for applying yourself as you've been taught by men of faith from Lower Manhattan. You've soaked up the gospel like a sponge and you've made heart decisions about what you believe. You get it—right from wrong.

"Don't misunderstand my Old South stories—southern people are by no means perfect, but the North just about destroyed our country, so I can't help feeling pity.

"Lincoln referred to it as 'The War of the Rebellion'. He allowed the war was all about slavery and illegal secession. Well, that was not the truth. *Official Records of War of the Rebellion* recorded that seventy to eighty percent of the Confederate soldiers and sailors who fought the war were not slave owners. It was Mr. Lincoln's driving desire to transform this country into an all-powerful Federal government, to break down the rule of law that gives our sovereign states a set of their own rights. My father, Albert Henry, wrote home that he was fighting for 'States Rights all the way' because it was the patriotic thing to do and he, along with men from the other ten southern sovereign states who fought, believed in it. He felt like it was a shame we had to fight for what was already settled in the Constitution and Bill of Rights, but when the time came, he willingly left the family and did what men do—he went to war. Until Lincoln came along, States Rights' heroes kept this government in check and this is what I want you to get. Plenty of men in the Republican Party are advocates for big government even now in 1887, but Lincoln had a lot of devious supporters from other countries, too. Men like Karl Marx and Frederick Engels. Remember those names, for you will see them again many times. They are communists who praised Lincoln for attacking the South for their stand on States' Rights. Lincoln was an ally of the Communist and Fascist groups, which was ludicrous, because they were not even American citizens. In fact, Karl Marx hopped from one country to another trying to find someone who would have him. He was born in the Kingdom of Prussia in 1818 and died in London in 1883 when he was just sixty-four years old. He lived in Germany, France, Belgium and the United Kingdom and by 1845 he was deemed stateless.

"Malachi, you and I are particular about our religion. It means everything to us, and we don't allow anyone to touch our belief system. Karl Marx said that *religion is the sigh of the oppressed creature, the heart of a heartless world, and the soul of soulless conditions. It is the opium of the people.* If we break this down, Malachi, we have to know that Marx is saying that what we hold dear as our belief in God and His Son, Jesus, is but a stupefying, highly addictive narcotic that has lulled us to sleep. According to Marx, Christians do not live in reality. Religion has doped us and duped us.

"The more I read, the more I know that Lincoln was dead wrong about the South. Malachi, from what you know so far, which do you logically think or know came first, the Union or the States or Colonies as they were first called?"

"Of course the States came first, one by one. That's just common sense."

"The smartest immigrant I know just answered correctly! But do you know that still there are people from all walks of life in America who don't know the answer to that question. Lincoln pretended he didn't know. He showed his lack of education or his stubbornness about the beginning of our country by declaring that the States of the Union were never sovereign, that the Union existed before the States, and that made the Union sovereign and not the individual States. It is not correct to speak of the United States as a country being sovereign—only the States within the Union are sovereign. It has to be about the people."

"This is all so interesting, Mr. Lee. There's so much to learn, and I'm proud to be hearing it from someone I trust, like you."

"Well, I am privileged to have a copy of the Constitution and the Bill of Rights, and I belabor my point. The Constitution does not declare the Union to be sovereign, but it does declare that sovereignty belongs to 'we the people' of the sovereign states. Lincoln denied this. He was wrong. He abused the Constitution whether out of ignorance or mean-spiritedness. Listen to this story, Malachi, and you can tell me how you feel.

"I know you've heard the song, 'The Star Spangled Banner'?"

"Yes sir. I love that song. It makes m' proud."

"Do you know who wrote that song, Malachi, and how long ago he wrote it?"

"No sir. I never thought about it."

"His name was Francis Scott Key. He was an American author and poet and he was a lawyer, born in Frederick County, Maryland. During the Anglo-American War of 1812, he watched the British bombardment of Fort McHenry in Maryland in 1814, and when he saw the American flag flying over the fort early that morning before the sun came up, he wrote a poem and published it. The poem was set to music, and with Key's words, it became known as *The Star-Spangled Banner*. Key owned slaves, but he freed them all long before the War Between the States. He kept one on his farm and paid him to be his foreman. He publicly criticized slavery and even gave free legal representation to those seeking their freedom.

"Now, this is the part I want you to understand. Almost fifty years later, Francis Scott Key's grandson, Francis Key Howard, was arrested and put in jail by military courts during the War Between the States for speaking out against Lincoln's war policy. He was imprisoned at Fort McHenry, that same place where his grandfather stood and watched the British bomb and burn as he wrote *The Star Spangled Banner*."

"Oh, my goodness!" Malachi could scarcely believe it. "So Lincoln's men arrested Mr. Howard and imprisoned him? Why?"

"Because Howard was the editor of the *Baltimore Exchange*, a newspaper that was sympathetic to the southern cause. Union General George B. McClellan ordered him arrested for writing an editorial critical of Lincoln's suspending the writ of *habeas corpus*. The Lincoln Radical Regime also arrested and imprisoned, without due process, the mayor of Baltimore, a Congressman, the police commissioner, and the entire city council. So Lincoln was invading the privacy of American citizens and shutting down newspapers, never giving them a chance to defend themselves, depriving them of the benefits of trial by jury. Howard spent fourteen months in Ft. McHenry prison then Ft. Lafayette in Lower New York Bay then Ft. Warren in Boston. His grandfather, Francis Scott Key, a prisoner on a British ship, had written that beautiful song. Can you imagine how his grandson felt, as he looked at that flag blowing in the wind at Ft. McHenry over fifty years later? Malachi, I say, what happened to our country in those four years of Lincoln's war was disgraceful."

"I'm so ashamed of Mr. Lincoln," said Malachi, tears rolling down his cheeks. "So ashamed."

"You know, it was one thing for England to invade our country, and it was wrong. They suffered and paid a price for that war. But for the President of the United States to call war on the legally seceded Confederate States of America was a grave mistake that cost the lives of over 620,000 men and boys from both sides, and—it cost Mr. Lincoln his own life.

"Well, Mr. Lincoln is gone now, but he had surrounded himself with what some call tyrants who felt the same way he did. Obviously, it was nothing for them to carry out his orders.

"And that's not all, Malachi. I tell you this because even now there are those who idolize Lincoln. Our liberties have been and continue to be attacked because of his decisions to put the Federal government and its demands before the rights of the States to choose.

"Karl Marx and Frederick Engels were enthusiastic supporters of Lincoln and his war. As you become more and more educated, you will find that the Union Army—Lincoln's Army and the Radical Republican Regime were tainted with Communists. Remember this name, Charles A. Dana. He was Assistant Secretary of War in Lincoln's cabinet. Lincoln's General Weydemeyer was a member of the Communist League of London with Marx and Engles. Dana and Weydemeyer were active in the Radical Party. They were responsible for getting Marx's *Communist Manifesto* published in the United States. These men were all lovers of Lincoln. Do you see what I'm saying, Malachi?

"It was the doctrine of States Rights for which the South fought that was under attack and the Communists helped clear the path for Lincoln and a supreme federal government. Sincerely speaking, I believe this country will never be the same because of the Radical Regime. I hope I'm wrong, but it seems there's always something brewing and it will one day surface its ugly head. Let's pray that it doesn't."

Chapter 18

On This Very Day—

Dawn came cold and sunny, Thanksgiving Day finding Lee and Malachi on the quiet streets of New York City, making their way down Broadway to the lowermost parts of Manhattan. Lee had not been to the Tavern since he came with the family many years before. He wondered if things had changed. He hoped not. He wanted Malachi to know as much about Gen. George Washington as he did about Robert E. Lee and Stonewall Jackson. George Washington was a southern gentleman, a true patriot, and his wife's great-granddaughter, Mary Anna Custis Randolph was—well she married Robert E. Lee. Fraunces Tavern had been as familiar to Gen. Washington as Mount Vernon, his Virginia home. Mr. Oscar Alexander had told the story to Lee Payne, for his British-American step-grandfather knew the history of Manhattan Island like the back of his hand.

To Lee's delight, the doors were open and the aroma was much like that at home in Sarepta on Thanksgiving Day. A huge butter-basted turkey, brown from the oven took center of the serving table, surrounded by vegetables of all sorts, cranberries, home-made bread, and sweet potato pie. Once again, it was rudimentary for Malachi, who was most thankful for the day at the tenements when he first laid eyes on Robert E. Lee Payne.

"Mr. Lee, I wonder what else I will learn today."

"I kind of wanted to apologize for overwhelming you with all the war history. There is so much good about our country, and we are both citizens of this beloved land. I just wanted you to know the history of the South *and* the North, and I definitely want it to be slanted toward the South. Only kidding! It's hard not to lean heavily toward my southern roots, recalling the heartbreak of the war years."

"I understand, Mr. Lee. Believe me, I feel like I'm part of y'r southern family, and when y' hurt, I hurt. Miss Rachel will be m' grandmother, too, and she lost .... All of y' did. I'm there with y' Mr. Lee. Right there with y'."

They were seated and the servers brought hot cups of coffee to their table, which Lee and Malachi knew would compliment everything on the long serving buffet. Malachi was going to learn something knew today. How to serve himself at a formal banquet. This was unusual for the Tavern, but the best way to serve many guests at one time. It suited Malachi, of course, and with a few quick hits with etiquette instruction, they were ready to serve their own plates.

"I saw that pumpkin pie, Mr. Lee. We're going to get to do it again, aren't we?"

"It looks that way, Malachi, unless you want to try something new and different."

They savored every bite, Malachi having chosen the sweet potato pie and another cup of coffee, and Lee began the history lesson.

"Almost on this very day, on November 25, 1783, the last of the British troops left New York City. Amazingly, they never attacked the City. I guess they loved frequenting the taverns too much to destroy them! A few days later, in early December, after the British had left American soil, Gen. George Washington invited his officers of the Continental Army to meet him in the Long Room of this very Tavern for a farewell gathering. He was about to take final leave of his troops and return to his home in Mt. Vernon, Virginia. He poured a little wine in their glasses and commenced to speak to them. Then he began to weep. Each officer took him by the hand, embraced their commander, and then weeping as if their hearts would break, drank their wine and left, a departure that went down in history as the most heartbreaking ever. That's how much love Gen. Washington had for his men and they for him. Now there's a real president, Malachi. Our first and best. And he was from where?"

"The South, Mr. Lee. The South!"

It was getting late and colder and almost dark when Lee and Malachi left Fraunces Tavern, heading north up Broadway to their homes.

"We have a lot to do, Malachi. I have already written Grandmother and Mr. Oscar telling them about you. I'm counting on Grandmother to tell my mother, Cassie, and my father, Jonathan. She will gladly do that. We have to move to our apartment, which will take nothing, really. We have little to take with us. We must plan for the wedding and the arrival of Miss Charlotte and her mother later in the month; we need to decorate for Christmas, quickly, and I have to prepare myself mentally to take on my new job after the wedding. If you think of anything else that needs to be on our list, please jot it down."

"Yes sir, Mr. Lee. And I was just thinking, maybe I should stay at McBurney's until school closes for the Christmas holidays."

"Excellent idea, Malachi. And I might as well stay at the Brownstone until then, too. That will save a few trips of running back and forth for both of us. By then, Grandmother and Mr. Oscar should be home for a few months. However, we can go ahead and move in and decorate for Christmas."

"I think we have a good plan," said Malachi.

It was daunting, but the list narrowed as the days passed. By December 1, Lee had received a letter from Oscar whose greeting was to him *and* Malachi. Carlisle handed it to Lee when he arrived at work early that morning.

"What a thoughtful thing to do," said Lee. He read the letter then handed it to Carlisle.

Written from Sarepta, Mississippi
Late November, 1887

Dearest Lee and Malachi,

Clearly these are exciting days for the two of you and for Miss Charlotte Jackson Elliott. Let me say that Grandmother Rachel and I are particularly excited about having you in our family, Malachi. We don't know all the details yet, but we are eagerly waiting the day when we will meet you face to face. Lee has told us all that is possible on a piece of white paper, but soon we will know what you look like, what your voice sounds like, how big or small you are, and none of that matters. It will just be icing on the cake. It is with joy that I, as an immigrant to this great country, welcome you on equal ground. We are European brothers, and let me assure you, these Paynes find no difference. They love any and everybody. 'Tis a grand triumph that you came ashore in New York Harbor and found your way into the heart and life of a southern man the likes of Robert E. Lee Payne. I can tell from his introduction of you that he loves you dearly and that he will faithfully care for you now and forever.

Lee, your grandmother and I will arrive in New York in time for your wedding, but shortly after Christmas, so do not worry. Go ahead and move into your new apartment whenever you are ready and just continue to go by the Brownstone two or three times a week. Pick up the milk and take it to your place.

We read your latest article in *The New York Elite Press* as it arrived by post in Sarepta just yesterday, and it was a fine one. Reading it from the newspaper is far better than reading the proof on telegraph paper. How proud we are of you! You are telling the story of the Old South, and 'tis music to our ears. We look forward to the next issues, and when I return, you and I can sit down and discuss your future as a permanent journalist for *The New York Elite Press*. That is to say, if you so desire.

All in the Sarepta connection send their love and best wishes for a beautiful wedding in The Central Park.

Cordially,
Oscar Alexander

"Yes, this is vintage Oscar Alexander," said Carlisle. "His way of welcoming Malachi and having him feel comfortable about meeting his new family. I would say things are going quite well, Lee. I knew from the day you told me the whole Malachi story that you chose to do the right thing for this young Irish immigrant, this former street urchin such as I. Have you heard from Immigration yet?"

"No, I have great expectations of hearing this week. Miss Benôit said it would be late November or early December. I had to go back to Immigration and sign a dozen papers so they could check me out. The only thing that concerns me is that I am a Democrat and my father and grandfather died fighting for the Confederacy. Miss Benôit did not seem to think that would matter. She said we were all Americans. I hope she's right."

"And you've got to remember, many New Yorkers are Democrats, too. We didn't like Lincoln's actions in our city any more than southerners did. So, I think you will be just fine. I hope you hear soon."

"Thanks, Brother! Me, too."

"Oh, and what's this about you joining the newspaper on a permanent assignment?"

"Yes, I focused on that a bit, too, now definitely pulled between the possibility and that of my commitment to building bridges and tall buildings in this growing City. I'm sure the fact that I've signed a contract for one year will enter into my thoughts and decisions."

"Yes, and I'm sure the answer will come. You know how much I would love to see you stay with us at the paper."

"And I've come to love the feel of pen and paper. Guess I'm that much like Rachel."

"There is no better journalist," said Carlisle.

Chapter

Unfinished Business—

As Lee Payne made preparations to settle permanently in a place that was as far removed from the Old South as he could possibly get, he began to have second thoughts. How could he conscientiously do this without betraying his heritage?

The South had not only lost the war, it had lost over a third of its men and boys. After the bugle had played the last tattoo and all was said and done at Appomattox Court House that day in April of 1865, those who were left dragged their disconsolate war-torn bodies along the dusty roads of the Southland, each to his old home place, and that on foot, most not knowing if it were still standing or if the North had completely destroyed it. Their bodies were bent, but they held their heads high, demonstrating their Christian faith, knowing beyond a reasonable doubt that they would be ridiculed and scorned by the North in the days and years to come. The memories of the war years, his father and his grandfather and all those who had lost their lives for *the Cause* haunted him. And Lee struggled to put away the painful thoughts.

He prayed for God to lead him into his future with Charlotte and Malachi, and if He so desired for Lee to have a change of direction that He would point the way. He owed it to those who made it possible for him to become educated in the building of bridges and buildings to make efforts in that direction. But maybe he could do two things at one time. His grandmother had always taught him to start walking toward his goals, using his talents and knowledge and trust God to make a way through the darkest night.

Thoughts of Gen. Robert E. Lee overwhelmed him at times. He had considered his warriors to be the finest that had ever donned a uniform and strapped on a squirrel rifle, and he once said they were *the noblest fellows the sun ever shone upon*. Furthermore, Lee Payne knew the General had called thousands of fighting Mississippi men and boys by a carefully chosen name—*My Mississippians*. That had included Lee's people, his devoted family members who gave their lives on the battlefield of Gettysburg.

He pulled his rig to the curb of the new apartment building, made several trips, taking things he had accumulated over the years, and the household necessities his grandmother had given him. It was not much, but he could not take it all at once. He rode the service elevator to the fourteenth floor. He would get this done and go to the newspaper where things were always lively, rejecting the thought of being alone today. He didn't like admitting that darkness had overtaken him, something he was not accustomed to. He would go to Hannigan's after his work day ended in hopes of continuing a conversation they had started several months ago. Lee would get as much of the war stuff off his mind as he could. For now, it was like unfinished business. He allowed writing the articles had dredged up intense feelings. Mr. Hannigan seemed to be like-minded about certain things. Maybe it was because he was Irish and he suffered the potato famine in Ireland, came to New York and opened the pub and in 1863, endured the Riots in Lower Manhattan.

"Irish coffee, Payne? Hold the whiskey but burn it, heavy cream and sugar, a little nutmeg grate."

"You always know, Mr. Hannigan. Thank you. I really need a good coffee today."

"What brings y' here—without Malachi, that is?" Hannigan wiped the bar and sat Lee's coffee down.

"I thought maybe you would tell me about the Draft Riots if you have time. Sometimes I can't get my mind off what happened, and knowing that New York was as affected as places like Shiloh, Tennessee, and Oxford, Mississippi, though not in the same way, is part of the mystery of what actually took place. Malachi told me parts of the story that concerned his papa."

Hannigan took a deep breath and spoke. "First of all, let me say that I have been reading y'r articles in *The Elite Press*, and I'm really impressed. Y're a good writer, Payne. I'm proud to know y'. Are y' going to put any of this into y'r next article?"

"Not if you don't want me to."

"Of course, I don't mind. Just don't quote me. Y' can go to Mr. Alexander's newspaper archives and confirm what I'm going to tell y'. There will not likely be a word's difference. It was in all the papers, but m' version of it will be much more exciting, because I was right in the middle of the war down here on the East Side.

"It was a military draft lottery imposed upon the country, and it stirred up the City of New York. I don't think anyone took into consideration the extent of the social divides in this City in those days. When all was said and done, the largest civilian insurrection in American history took place right here. There was an involvement that rose to the surface when it all got started. The wealthy influence, the Africans, and the Irish immigrants. I know, for I am one m'self. I was just not involved in the uprising. And the biggest problem was that war itself."

"What do you mean by that?"

"Well, be patient. I'm going to tell y'," said Hannigan.

Lee laughed, promising to listen and not get ahead of the story.

"New York City is a big place. When the war started in 1861, our merchants and banks, and other businesses, were affected by the loss of southern opportunities. It didn't take long for anyone with good sense to see the agricultural South was being depleted of everything and that was affecting the North. The Mayor at the time was Fernando Wood. He literally called for the City to secede from the Union."

"You don't mean it," shouted Lee.

"I do, indeed," said Hannigan.

"Why, I never knew the City threatened secession. You only think of states seceding."

"That's true, but just look at the population of New York. We must be larger than some states in number. Immigrants were coming in by the score, and we had our own worries. We didn't need those political issues adding to our economic and cultural problems.

"The poor people saw no benefit to what was happening, just the rich people."

"Why was that?" asked Lee.

"The wealthy wer' getting even richer because the spoils of battle wer' going to them. The draft lottery allowed the wealthy men to buy their way out of the draft by paying a three hundred dollar fee. The lottery exempted Africans because they were not citizens. They didn't have to register for the draft and they didn't have to pay. Politicians got involved, the Democrats crying the loudest because of the impact on the poor class of people. It was a mixed up mess.

"Well, when the list came out, y' can imagine what happened. People began to protest in a big movement. The crowds gathered, some of them armed with weapons. Even a volunteer fire company got mad about the drafting of their chief, of all things. They commenced to fist fighting, smashed windows in the building where the officials had set up to draft the men, broke into the building and destroyed their equipment.

"And get this. It will interest y', Payne. The mob targeted the newspapers that wer' in favor of the war, of course."

"Which newspapers," asked Lee?

"I know one was *The New York Tribune*."

"Horace Greeley, huh?"

"Yes. A liberal Republican and an abolitionist. Early morning of July 13, protestors pounced on the Lower East Side where all the newspapers are and the staff people fired on them. All kinds of havoc broke out.

"It rained all night and the next day they just kept on destroying and looting, making it hard for the police to get things under control. Then they started attacking African immigrants. The politicians squabbled about what to do. They tried a little of everything, including offering low-interest loans to buy draft exemptions. And the riots spread to Brooklyn and Staten Island. By this time, the mob was largely Irish Catholic men, and the City involved the Archbishop to make an appeal for peace.

"I think this was the saddest thing, and it may affect y', Payne. Around mid-day on July 16, over four thousand Federal soldiers marched through the City straight from the Gettysburg battlefield. They ended the New York City Draft Riots that day."

Lee dropped his head in surprise. "The longer I live, and I'm still young, the more I learn of that Civil War. Thank you for telling me the real story of what happened. I didn't know the extent, and I had no idea that Union soldiers from the Gettysburg battle came to end the fight in New York City. Maybe one of those soldiers killed my father in the Peach Orchard, or my grandfather in the Railroad Cut at Gettysburg. Sometimes it gets really close to home, Mr. Hannigan."

"I know, Payne. I know. I hope this has not stirred y'r emotions even more."

"No. Don't think that. I asked you to tell me the story, and I appreciate it. More of the pieces of the puzzle now come together. I knew that some New Yorkers didn't like Lincoln for many and various reasons. The more I learn about the man, the sicker I become."

Chapter

Intense Feelings—

Christmas came to New York City. Lee and Malachi spent the holidays in the new apartment putting their belongings away and purchasing a bit of food for the cupboard and ice box. They dared not cook, but snacked on fruit and cheese and crusty bread from the corner market. Rachel had taught Lee how to make the sandwich with tomato, cheese and mayonnaise. He could do it with no craft required. Most of this kind of living was new to the boys. They had never heard of a snack, one hailing from the poor Deep South, the other from the pit of poverty in the tenements. They quickly learned the route to the market by way of the trolley. After only a few days of this luxury living, Malachi returned to McBurney's for the time being, and Lee to the Brownstone.

The list was becoming burdensome for Lee, and he wished for Charlotte. She would know what to do. He rode Dixie early of a morning, Fifth Avenue to Thirty-Seventh Street and The Brick Presbyterian Church. He loved this church that represented so much history dating back to

1767. Since then, its doors had been opened continuously except for the years of the Revolutionary War when British Forces commandeered it for a hospital and later, they used it as a jail. He claimed it as his own now, and hoped Charlotte would love it as much as he did. Rachel and Mr. Oscar had been faithful members since their marriage. They had dearly loved Reverend Gardiner Spring who pastored from 1810 to his death in 1873. Rachel still spoke of him with love and admiration and she would never forget his sermon on "Cherished Sins," which she had lovingly passed on to her grandson, Lee.

He tied Dixie to the post in front of the red brick church, walked gingerly across the creaky wood floors through the old sanctuary to Reverend Van Dyke's study at the back, wondering if there were any dead buried in these walls like those churches in Lower Manhattan. Lee tapped on the door, hoping the pastor was there. In a twinkling, he opened the door and received Lee with a big smile.

"'Tis happy I am to see you, Lee. What do you hear from your Grandmother Rachel and Mr. Alexander?"

"They're well, thank you. They'll be returning from the South in just days now."

"In time for your wedding, I'm sure."

"Yes sir, and I wanted to make certain you have all the details. Charlotte and I chose to have the ceremony at Bow Bridge in The Central Park if that is acceptable with you."

"I think that is a splendid idea, Lee. And I hope you plan to play the music on your violin."

"I have considered it, sir." Lee smiled broadly, for he wouldn't miss that opportunity. "I only wish my uncles could be here. There would then be five of us Mississippi Boys. It would be the finest music ever played at an outdoor winter wedding, if I do say so."

"I have no doubt about that. Your grandmother obviously taught her boys well."

"She did, indeed. Oh, and Pastor, I do hope a lively version of 'Dixie' would not offend you. I promise to wait until the ceremony has ended."

"What a novel idea. I hope you will not change your mind about that."

"No sir. I'm probably the most unashamed southern boy in New York City."

"You southern boys amaze me, Lee. We should all possess your audacity. It would make the world a better place."

"Thank you, sir, for all your kindness in performing our ceremony. I will leave it all to you."

Lee reached for his coat, and shaking Reverend Van Dyke's hand, he properly bid him good-day and took leave of the meeting house.

Lee reined Dixie in at The Central Park Stables and hitched her to his rig. He drove to the Custom House, hopeful that Miss Benôit had good news for him. It was hard for him to believe when this all got started, the days were warm and spring had brought new hope and promise. Now winter was coming on and the streets were already covered with a thin layer of snow. In just a few moments he would know something concerning Malachi.

He approached the entry booth and asked for Miss Benôit, giving his name and Malachi's. In moments, the lovely French lady in black greeted him with hand extended and a broad smile.

"I'm really glad to see you, Mr. Lee Payne."

"It's great to see you, too, Miss Benôit. You look cheerful. Could that possibly mean …"

"As a matter of fact, I posted a letter to you just two days ago, which you should receive in a few days, but never mind that now, for I can tell you, I was simply requesting your return to see us. And I do have good news for you. The Immigration Board has granted you custody of Malachi. And that is even without the consent of Miss Charlotte Jackson Elliott because of Malachi's age. And if you want to sign the papers, he will become your son effective on this date."

Lee was in momentary shock, though it was the news he had hoped for. This would seal everything, and as suddenly as Miss Benôit said the words, depression lifted as if by Divine Hand.

"That's exactly what it was! Jesus has lifted my burden. It was not for me, it was for Malachi. Oh, pardon me, Miss Benôit. I was just rejoicing. The Lord God has granted my heart's desire. Yes, yes, I'll gladly sign the papers. And Miss Benôit, may I give Malachi my name?"

"Of course, we would like for you to do that. I can draw up the final papers including your name. That is, if you think Malachi would like that."

"Yes, yes! I believe—I know he would like that. Malachi O'Malley Payne … A great name …"

"Then that's what I'll do right now."

Miss Benôit began filling out the final agreement papers for Lee to sign. As with Malachi's immigration documents, she had the papers printed in calligraphy and presented them to Robert E. Lee Payne, father of Malachi O'Malley Payne.

"I hope you will visit us from time to time, Mr. Payne, for we will certainly miss you and Malachi."

"And we will miss you, as well, Miss Benôit. You have helped change our lives and we are grateful."

Lee left the Custom House smiling. Without a thought for anything else, he tapped Dixie and sped north and eastward toward Hannigan's where Malachi would be working. He tied the rig at the curb and bounded into the old Irish pub.

"Where's Malachi, Cavanaugh?"

"He just finished, I think. He'll be out here in a few minutes. You're spirited about something, Payne."

"Indeed! Just wait until you hear."

Within minutes, Malachi joined Lee at the counter, all clean and ready to follow Mr. Lee wherever that might be. He could tell something was going on that obviously featured him. Cavanaugh and Hannigan were present for whatever was being announced.

"What is it, Mr. Lee?"

Lee held up the documents and then spread them on the wood counter. Malachi took one look and broke into a big smile and as usual tears rolled down his cheeks.

"This is it, eh? And what's this? Y' gave me y'r name?"

"That is, only if that's the way you want it. Miss Benôit said we can change that part if we do it quickly."

"Oh, no! I would never want to change m' new name. I think that's the way m' mother would have wanted it. To know that I have a family that loves m' enough to give m' their name. Mr. Lee, I can never repay y' for what y've done."

"Then could you just please call me something more endearing than Mr. Lee?"

They laughed and Malachi confessed that he had picked a name long ago.

"How about Papa?"

"That's exactly what I hoped for. I know I could never take your papa's place, but I gladly accept that and hope I can be a real father to you in his absence, Malachi. You can always count on me."

Chapter 21

A Little Ragged Box—

Speaking out loud helped Lee to remember what he needed to do next, though it made him feel obtuse. "I don't care," he said. "This has to be done. I guess I could use a piece of white paper, but at this point, I would probably still be talking to myself. Just one more thing. I must purchase some linens for the apartment and take them over."

He knew Charlotte was bringing her trunk, and hopefully it would be laden with things for the apartment. Her mother had shared. He knew that much.

He took the elevator to the fourteenth floor and lugged his packages into the apartment. The fragrance like a winter song swirled about him. What was it? Apples? He had not been back since he and Malachi left after Christmas. There in the living room was a beautiful Christmas tree decorated with jewels from The Central Park. Evergreen, holly berries, and there they were, fresh cold red apples in the silver bowl he recognized. Rachel had given it to him from the attic at the newspaper. His first and only wedding gift. Malachi had polished it and filled it with ruby red apples.

Yes, Malachi had been there, and what an awesome sight! Lee wondered how he did it all and came to the conclusion that possibly Cavanaugh had helped him with the tree and Central Park decorations.

Lee put the new white linens on the bed and turned it down with the beautiful hand sewn quilt he had brought from Rachel's stash. He must remember to tell her. He thought to dangle a bit of Malachi's mistletoe at the light in the ceiling. His bride would love it, even though it was already past Christmas. It was part of the plan.

He placed the towels in the bathing room, put new linens on Malachi's bed, and was done, all he had to offer, and it was perfect. The house was wintry cold and the apples would be fine and fragrant until he carried Charlotte across the threshold on January 4.

"Thank you, Lord—and my son, Malachi!"

As he started to leave, Lee glanced once more at the table where the cold red apples rested in the silver bowl. Something unusual lay beside it—a little familiar ragged box, which he did not notice earlier, tied with string and under it a piece of white paper on which someone had written a note. He picked it up. 'Twas Malachi's handwriting of these words, "Papa, this is for y' to give to Miss Charlotte on y'r wedding day. I know we never found her a wedding ring to go with the beautiful diamond, which y' suffered pain and agony to defend, and I would like for her to have m' mother's ring if y' would allow it. 'Tis m' most valued possession, and there is no one on the face of the earth that I love more than y' and Miss Charlotte. I polished it and 'tis shiny still, so m' thinks it will suffice. I hope y' will think the same. All m' best for all y've been to me." It was signed Malachi O'Malley Payne.

Tears rolled down Lee's face. "This kid never quits," he said aloud, choking and crying. "God in Heaven, I love him."

Charlotte and her mother boarded the Pullman in Lexington bound for New York City. Snow had fallen all night with promise of many more inches over the next few hours as they traveled northeastward.

"It's a good thing we allowed ourselves extra days before the wedding, Charlotte, just in case the snow slows us down for arrival into the City."

"You're right about that, Mama."

Reluctantly, Charlotte added, "You know we'll soon be entering Union country, Mama. A place you've never been."

Margaret tightened her lips and did not smile.

"You need not get the idea I will ever be anything but a real daughter of the Confederacy. Papa left us a remarkable legacy. He lived the war and died with the greatest general that ever lived, Stonewall Jackson. We hold our heads high and will never forget."

"I know that, Charlotte, but New York City—how much more Yankee does it get? Why, Ulysses S. Grant is buried there. Will there be a time when people will find out you're the daughter and Lee's the son of Confederate War dead?"

"It's not really like that anymore, Mama. You'll see. And if you ever want to come and live with Lee and Malachi and me,—well, you know you can do that."

"I'll adapt, but I'll never leave the South," said Margaret Elliott. "You will bury me in Lexington, Virginia, Charlotte. And don't let that announcement bother you, for I am ready and prepared to go Home; that is, to my final Home, where Jesus is, and where Papa is."

Charlotte bit her lip and swallowed hard to keep from crying.

"I know, Mama. You're like Robert E. Lee. He turned down a commission with the Union Army because he could never raise his sword against his native Virginia. And I know you're ready to go to Heaven, but please, not yet. Now—let's talk about good things that are about to happen here in this life."

"Malachi!" said Margaret. "Let's talk about my grandson. I can't wait to lay eyes on that boy."

"You're in for a real treat, Mama. He's from another world, one that makes the South pale in comparison as it concerns poverty. But you would never know it. He's self-educated, which makes him a novelty, and now he's being further educated by loving pastoral scholars who are heaping spiritual and textbook knowledge upon him daily. And with Lee Payne's layer of social graces and a godly blanket of kindness covering him like a baby chick in a warmer, Malachi will not fail. I'm so proud of him. Besides that, you're going to love his Irish accent and genuine warmth. And he's the entertainer just being himself. I'm like you, I can't wait to see him— again."

Charlotte laid her book down and glanced at her mother who sat in the seat next to her. She had fallen asleep. H*ow lovely, thought Charlotte, and I'm going to miss her immensely.* She did not want to wake her, but at the same time, she suddenly had the depth of feeling that something dreadful could happen to her mother and she would be far away. Charlotte, overcome with emotions, leaned back in her seat and let the tears roll down her cheeks.

Margaret Elliott was a beautiful woman, the widow of a Confederate Captain who fought in the Stonewall Jackson Brigade. He took a musket shot to the chest at the Battle of Chancellorsville and died on the field. His death had taken a toll on Margaret, and Charlotte knew it, though her mother, like thousands of southern women, had tried to keep her feelings private. In the days prior to the train ride to New York City, Margaret had visited her family physician of many years. Would her health sustain the long ride and the stress of her daughter's wedding? She sat in the cheerful receiving room of Benjamin Walker, M.D. whom she had known for forty years. She knew every drape that hung from the massive windows in the old clinic, every piece of furniture. The antiseptic smell was familiar and made her feel comfortable. Nothing much had changed through the years. She waited her turn until he appeared and motioned for her to join him.

"Margaret, I don't have to tell you how fragile you are. There is no medication that I can send with you. Your heart has endured many years of stress since the Captain died in the war."

"And you've done an excellent job of helping me through it, Dr. Walker."

"Give yourself credit for most of that. How you've lived your life has made the difference, Margaret. But this trip is going to stretch your stamina. You will likely see your strength start to fail early in the afternoons, and you must take the time to rest. I don't advise that you go, but I know you're going anyway, because Charlotte needs her mother at a time like this."

"This is something I have to do, Ben. She's my only child, and if I can make it through her wedding and back home to Lexington, I'll be happy."

"Then all I can do is wish you God's best for the journey and beg you to avoid all strenuous activities."

"I will, and don't worry over me, Ben. You have other patients who need you."

"None that mean as much to me as you and Charlotte."

She touched her mother gently.

"What is it, Charlotte, dear?"

"Mama, do you think time heals a broken heart?"

"Well, yes. I know it does, Charlotte. I'm the perfect example of that, and I would hope that you have healed from your father's death in the war. You were so young. Why do you ask?"

"Stay with me in New York City, Mama."

"What? No, Charlotte. You know I can't do that."

"But Mama, you're going to be alone, and you're not getting any younger."

"I was old when I gave birth to you, Charlotte, and now you are nearing thirty."

"Papa died at Chancellorsville in May of 1863. I'm a year older than Lee."

"Why are you talking like this, Charlotte?"

"Because I want you to stay."

"I will stay one week, and then I must get back to Lexington."

"Do you think badly of me for leaving you, Mama? For if you do, I cannot bear it."

"Of course not, Charlotte. I'm happy for you. You know that. I've always wanted you to marry someone who loves you and will take care of you. I would not rob you of happiness nor think you should stay home the rest of your life. That would not be natural. Remember, I left all to follow your papa. How could I expect you to do less?"

"I'm not worried about me, Mama, I'm worried about you."

"Let's stop talking about it, dear. Everything is going to be fine."

"So many have died, Mama. Please … please don't die."

Charlotte began to shake, trying hard to stifle the tears, but to no avail.

"Charlotte, you're going to have Lee and Malachi. They're young and full of life. They will make you laugh and enjoy happy times. Just wait, you'll see."

"I don't know if I can be a good wife and mother."

"Well believe me, you cannot learn in a single day, but the things I've taught you—will you not put them into practice?"

"I promise to try, Mama."

"You won't fail."

"I'm sorry, Mama. I'm just having a moment of wondering about what the future holds. Everything will be so different without you—without all I've been used to when it comes to my mama."

"Don't you suppose the same is true for Lee? Don't borrow from the sunshine, Charlotte."

"Yes, ma'am."

As Charlotte and her mother traveled, a train from Memphis was on its last leg of journey and would roll into the depot within minutes, that is, if the train happened to be on time. Lee and Malachi were there to meet its passengers, wondering who, if any, would have traveled with Grandmother Rachel and Mr. Oscar. It would be a surprise if others had made the trip from Sarepta with them.

Excitement had escalated for Malachi over the last few days and weeks. He hardly knew how to respond without becoming emotional. A new place to live, a new papa, a family he had never met, and later in the day, Miss Charlotte would arrive accompanied by his new Grandmother Margaret. Lee perceived Malachi was about to have a conniption.

The train had always fascinated Lee. It brought visions of his father, hopping the freight cars with a hundred other soldiers. Rachel had told him all she knew of that story. The men had walked for hours in the cold of winter. From Grenada through the north and eastern part of Mississippi, across the middle of Tennessee, and into the Commonwealth of Kentucky where they took the cars that night. Going to fight a war, and his father was only seventeen years old. Lee never got to talk to him about it. Maybe his father thought the sounds to be like a song with its own idiom, verses written to the grinding of the wheels, understood only by someone longing to be aboard or impatiently waiting for a loved one to step off the car and look both ways. For Lee it was like that. A language all its own, a storied account written in a secret dialect.

The lonesome whistle of the Pullman and the yellow light in a foggy day and thoughts of his father in the mountains of Kentucky resting on the cars stirred his emotions, and under his feet he could feel the rumble on the rails a mile away. *The little things make life better for me, he thought. I hope Papa felt the same way.*

Lee shook himself back to more recent thoughts of when he and the Mississippi Boys had stepped down to this same platform and surprised Rachel. Mr. Oscar had arranged the grand reunion with all the Sarepta connection—friends and family. Lee had this same feeling in the pit of his stomach, only this time, he was there to greet the portion of his family who would be arriving for his wedding. He was resigned to the probability that no other family members would be with Rachel and Mr. Oscar.

"Malachi, isn't this just so much excitement?"

"Oh, Papa. I feel like I'm about to explode with joy. And look at the snow. We're getting just what y' wanted. A nice covering for the Bow Bridge, I'm sure."

"They—whoever is on this train, are going to love you, son. You look like a million dollars today. With your long trousers and Navy peacoat. And, yes, your Irish apple newsboy cap. There is no mistaking your Irish descent, which makes me happy."

The engine forced a final thick cloud of steam beneath the iron wheels, like a giant whale out of water, and the Pullman chugged slowly into the station and stopped, the lonesome sound continuing for a few moments. It, too, ceased, and the Conductor gave instructions for the passengers to collect their belongings and step down to the platform. Lee and Malachi could hear the transition of train sounds being passed to its passengers scurrying about, the harmony ending and the cacophony beginning.

"Let's walk down the platform and then back up until we see someone we know," said Lee.

Malachi stood as close as he could get to his papa, measuring almost the height of Lee, although there was no other resemblance.

And then Rachel stepped off the train first.

"That's her, Malachi, your Grandmother Rachel. Go to her."

"But what if she doesn't know m'."

"Oh, she will know you."

Malachi picked up his pace and approached the frail gray-haired, but stunningly beautiful, woman. He put both arms around her and kissed her lovely cheeks, one at a time.

"Hello, Grandmother Rachel," he said, tears forming in his Irish blue eyes.

"Hello, Great-grandson Malachi O'Malley. I am so happy to finally lay eyes on you." She held him by the shoulders and lovingly pushed him back from her so she could see his handsome face. "I saw you from the window and I knew you—I knew you, and my heart filled with even more joy."

"Yes ma'am, Grandmother."

Rachel turned aside and caught Oscar's hand and pulled him close. "This is your Great-grandfather Oscar, Malachi."

Malachi extended his hand and stepped in close to the gentleman. He was tall and with a commanding presence. He reached to embrace Malachi.

"'Tis nice to meet y', sir."

"Likewise, Malachi. Our family welcomes you with open arms."

"Yes, sir, Mr. Oscar. And I've some wonderful news for later."

"I don't know if I can wait, son."

"I feel the same way, sir."

Lee properly greeted his grandparents and just so soon, Rachel pointed to the next car where an entourage was descending, gathering on the platform. Lee was now in utter astonishment. He ran to his mother, Cassie, and his father, Jonathan—and behind them, the other Mississippi Boys—Isaac, Joab, and Samuel.

"We had to leave the other women behind," said Jonathan. "There are so many young'uns, you know. They all wanted to be here and they send their love to you both."

Lee could see that Jonathan was using his cane. His heart pounded momentarily, but he had heard his father's voice, and he knew everything was going to be fine.

"I'm still in shock, Papa," he said. "How come I didn't figure this out? And here—here is my son, Malachi O'Malley, and as of this week, he legally bears our name—another Payne boy!"

They all hovered around Malachi, Cassie hugging and kissing her new grandson.

Lee stood aside and watched as Malachi made him so proud. "God made him to be a Payne," he whispered, tears rolling down his cheeks.

Rachel lifted her hand, begging a little silence. "All of you get your baggage, don't forget your violins, and we will hail some rides to the Brownstone. You're all staying with us. We've plenty of room. Some of us can ride with Lee and Malachi. Now, the question is—do you all want to come back and be here to greet Charlotte and Mrs. Elliott when they arrive? We have a few hours."

They agreed unanimously to return as a family.

Lee's head was spinning. As was Malachi's, who had never known family of any sort except his mother. This was splendid. He hoped he would find his usual words in response to all the southern hospitality that his new relatives brought with them from Sarepta. He dearly loved it.

Chapter 22

The Window Faces Broadway—

The Payne family made their way back to the train station late in the afternoon of New Year's Eve. Lee was smiling broadly, happy that he would see Charlotte in a matter of minutes and that she would have the pleasure of meeting his Sarepta family for the first time. It would be just awful if he had forgotten anything. At the same time, how could it matter now? He had run out of time. The next few days he would spend entertaining his family and friends, while at the same time being mindful of Malachi who was not used to large crowds of any sort. In the past, before Lee came along, it would have been nothing for him to avoid a crowd on the filthy streets of the East Side by simply boarding his Boneshaker and riding someplace, any place, where no people had gathered. But he had fit right in with the Mississippians this afternoon, and Lee was sure the same would be true with Charlotte's mother.

The train rumbled in the distance, his heart beating fast, slowing only as it arrived in the station and came to a dead stop. He took a deep breath. *Calm me, Lord, he prayed. I desire to enjoy this time of my life, but my emotions loathsomely interfere.*

"Malachi, when Grandmother Elliott steps down with Charlotte, please run to her and escort her? Because you know I'm going to be running to—"

"To Miss Charlotte, I know."

"Yes, indeed. Just introduce yourself and chat with Grandmother. She will love that, I'm sure."

Malachi, not knowing who was filled with the most anxiety, drew in a deep breath and stammered a moment. "Yes, yes sir, Papa. I hope I can do this."

"I have no worries, Malachi. Just be your gentlemanly self."

"Yes sir."

The family drew near, a crowd of twelve including Dan and his sons, who were always faithfully present and ready to assist the family to the carriages. When Charlotte stepped off the train with her mother, Lee caught his breath. He ran to her, and as he always did, he lifted her into his arms and swung her around and kissed her. The Mississippi Boys cheered, fully aware that Lee had made the choice of a lifetime, a beautiful southern woman, and Mrs. Elliott was equally as beautiful. Malachi did his job in style, and with much class, he greeted the lovely lady, properly holding to her hand as she descended to the platform.

"Grandmother Margaret?"

"You have to be Malachi!" she said. "I'm so happy to meet you, my dear grandson."

"Yes ma'am, Grandmother. I hope y' don't mind if I call y' Grandmother."

"It thrills me no end," she said, smiling broadly. "I was hoping you would."

"Come, I believe y' need to meet the Payne family, too."

Malachi took her to the family members, and calling each by name, which he had committed to memory just hours before, he introduced her.

Lee whispered to Charlotte, "Do you see what your son is doing? And by the way, let me be the first to tell you, Malachi belongs to us. I signed the papers with Miss Benôit a few days ago, and he is our son."

"Oh, thank God," said Charlotte, overjoyed at the news. "This is a magnificent wedding gift, Lee. And Mama already loves him, I can tell you that."

New Year's Eve brought supreme happiness to the Brownstone with Oscar and Rachel creating their own manner of celebrating family, friends, and new beginnings. Lee allowed Malachi was no longer apprehensive about being an outsider to this large and animated family, but heaven knows, he wanted to fit in without being obnoxious. He hardly knew what to do.

"Mr. Lee, I can stay at McBurney's until the wedding day," he said. "That way y' can be with y'r family more."

"No, Malachi! They are your family, too, and we all want you here with us."

"Well, that's exactly what I want to do, but I'm willing to make room for the others."

"Charlotte and Grandmother Margaret are staying at Gilsey House. They're tired from the journey, and we all have a big day tomorrow and then the next day at the Bow Bridge. Tonight, Dan is driving all us Mississippi Boys to the Battery to watch the fireworks and you are one of us. In fact, you can ride on the driver's bench with Dan and Samuel if you want to, and Sam will tell you all about us, me and him, that is, how we grew up together, two poor little southern wretches with no papa after the war, just like you, Malachi."

Malachi smiled broadly. He had never watched the fireworks up close over the harbor, only from a rooftop on the East Side tenements, and never with—a family.

"And, Malachi, you just called me Mr. Lee—"

"Oh, forgive me, Papa. I'm a little nervous."

Dan drove Charlotte and her mother to Gilsey House. He offered his arm to Margaret Elliott and escorted her to the elevator. She clung to him, hardly able to walk without help. Charlotte could see that her mother was very tired. It had been a long journey.

"I'll take my leave now, Miss Charlotte," he said. "If you needs me for anything, jes' let Mas Oscar know."

"Thank you, Dan. You've been so kind. Could you just help Mama up the elevator and into the room? I fear she is worn completely out."

"Yas'm. Then I'll get yo' baggage to the room and let you be. I be back to fetch you for the weddin' on January 3, which be a Sunday."

Charlotte's heart raced at the thought. She, too, was tired from the day's activities, but thoughts of the wedding gave her renewed energy. She would be able to help her mother once Dan got her to the room.

"Mama, I'll turn back this wonderful bed and you can climb right in. It's time for you to get off your feet and have a nice rest."

"I'll not argue with that, Charlotte. I cannot begin to tell you how weary I am."

"Doesn't this fire feel good and warm? Gilsey House is amazing. And I can go downstairs and get you some food if you're hungry." Charlotte chattered nervously.

"It's all lovely, dear, and I'm not the least bit hungry. The food at the Alexander's home was all I need for the night. You'll have to tell me how they put that interesting little feast together on such short notice."

"It's called the corner market, Mama. New York City has an amazing overabundance of every kind of food imaginable, and some unimaginable!"

"Well, I will look forward to breakfast in that window in the morning, and whatever it is, I'm sure it will suit me."

"That window faces Broadway, Mama. You're going to love it when I pull back the drapes in the morning. It's a far cry from what we're used to in Virginia. Tomorrow will be a free day for us, and you can rest to your heart's content, enjoying the hustle and bustle of holiday traffic from the window on Broadway. It's very entertaining, almost as interesting as a Broadway show, and much better than being out in that traffic. New York celebrates its holidays from Thanksgiving to New Year's, non-stop."

Chapter 23

Filled with Splendor—

The joyful noise emanating from the Brownstone on the Upper East Side of Manhattan was almost deafening, but the neighbors knew—they knew it was the wedding day of Mr. Alexander's grandson and that the house was crowded with southern guests, preparing to board the three rigs that stretched the length of the apartment building across from The Central Park. Carlisle Peterson, and his wife, Kathryn, had arrived early and placed the wreaths and white ribbons on the horses, a surprise for Lee and Charlotte. The Payne Boys—Jonathan, Isaac, Joab, Samuel, Lee and Malachi boarded the first carriage with the violins securely fastened in the trunk on the service seat. Carlisle and Kathryn, Oscar and Rachel, and Margaret Elliott, boarded next, and in the last carriage, Charlotte and Cassie, Charlotte wearing her beautiful white wedding dress and shivering in the wintry morning. She reached for the lovely white fleece blanket and covered herself and Cassie. Dan and his sons, each dressed to the hilt in top hats and black suits, climbed to the drivers' benches and the wedding party proceeded.

The Bow Bridge was covered with a thin layer of snow and the naked trees that hovered about in The Lake were laced with ice, nature's wedding decorations to this Victorian cast-iron beauty built with classical Greek refinement in 1862, just one year after the war began. Lee and Malachi could not have picked a more beautiful setting.

What! Had the entire newspaper shut down? For there were faces of so many friends who had gathered on the Bridge. And so it had, for Oscar Alexander had ordered it. Fifteen pressmen and journalists surrounded the wedding party as they arrived, one carriage behind the other onto the Bridge. The Payne men each took their violins from the trunk and began to tune up. The lonesome sounds swelled and resounded over the snow covered park, through the naked trees and across The Lake. And Lee was right, there was nothing like it. Beautiful strains of hymns and favorite songs of the South. When they played, "There's a land that is fairer than day" Cassie leaned toward Charlotte and said, "That's the song the boys played at their brother, Benjamin's, funeral. Of course, that was before Albert Henry and I married, the year the war broke out. Henry and I had just fallen in love. We were so young."

Tears were streaming down Cassie's cheeks.

"I'm sorry, Charlotte. It just brought back so many memories. I do hope one day you can get to Sarepta and see some of the places where the boys grew up. A far cry from New York City, that's for sure."

"I want to do that as soon as we can, Cassie. I hope you don't mind if I call you Cassie. You're so young and I hope we can be more than in-laws together."

"I wouldn't have it any other way," said Cassie.

"I think we're supposed to stay in the carriage until everyone else has gathered. Then you will go first, and I'll come behind you. To have been a small wedding, it has turned into a spectacular event, which makes me happy."

"You and Lee deserve it," said Cassie. "Lee has told us all about you in letters. We know that you lost your papa to the war like Lee did. You have a lot in common. And now you have this wonderful Malachi in your lives. What more could you ask for?"

Charlotte knew Cassie was right about Lee. He was her heart's desire. And to have Malachi, too—well, she would not have time to be lonely. She tried hard to suppress the tears, but she couldn't stop thinking of her mother and how that part of her life was, for all practical purposes, over. Nothing would ever be the same.

"I need to take one day at a time, don't I, Cassie?"

"Yes, indeed, Charlotte. I can only imagine your thoughts. Lee is going to take really good care of you. It's within these Payne boys to do that, and it's generational. Rachel has taught them well, and they fought a war with one of the best men I've ever known, their Papa."

Charlotte smiled and nodded not wanting to cry.

"The violin music—" said Cassie. "I will never forget this. Can you see, Charlotte?"

"Barely, but I can hear it. It's remarkably beautiful. I knew but could never have fathomed the depth of talent in this family. Who's going to tell us when to go?"

"Probably Kathryn. I hear she is the organizer of the family, and I think of her and Carlisle as family members because of what the boys told me when they were here several years ago. You know, Carlisle is to Mr. Alexander what Malachi is to you and Lee. He came along at a crucial time for both Oscar and Carlisle, a time when they needed each other."

The Payne family began to exit their carriages, the next chapter of their lives unfolding. They took their places, with the newsmen, proofers and printers, around the wedding party and family. Malachi stood beside Lee, as close as he could get and they waited for the violins to play *The Wedding March*. Malachi could see Hannigan and Cavanaugh from where he stood. Faithful friends, he thought, and smiled broadly then lifted his hand in a little wave, to which they responded.

"I hear it, Charlotte? It's time for us to step out and find our way to your beloved's side. Oh, don't cry, dear."

"I can't help it, Cassie. I cry about everything."

"I'm glad to hear that, actually. Now I do not feel alone."

And so instead, they laughed and started their walk toward the wedding party. Cassie made her way up the slight incline of Bow Bridge.

Jonathan's heart beat fast when he saw her, as he remembered the day he took the precious bride that had belonged to his brother, Albert Henry, and pledged to do as Henry had begged in a letter that he left in Jonathan's haversack before he was killed at Gettysburg. Memories flooded Jonathan, and he leaned heavily on his cane. He had promised Henry, posthumously, that he would take care of his wife and their son, Robert E. Lee Payne, for as long as he lived. And so Jonathan, who had never been one to shed a tear, struggled to suppress the desire.

Charlotte paused and kissed her mama, noticing the tears in her eyes and the far-away look. Jonathan took the bride's arm and walked the distance to present her to Lee, then returned to stand with his mother, Rachel. The little wedding party of four stood close as Rev. Van Dyke took up his Bible and began the ceremony.

Malachi listened to every word the preacher was saying. He understood. He had never been this proud in his life, proud to be a follower of Christ, proud to be an American, proud to be the son of Lee and Charlotte Payne. He entered into the message of love and redemption and promise and faithfulness of which Rev. Van Dyke spoke. Jesus would be the head of this family; and in his heart of hearts he pledged, he vowed, that he would do everything to make Lee and Charlotte proud. He pledged as a son to be their protectorate, to do the things their fathers, who had died prematurely in the war, might have done, as God would allow him.

He reached in his pocket and took out the ring Lee had given him earlier that morning, he kissed it, as if to say farewell, and handed it to Lee, though Charlotte had no idea Malachi was giving her his mother's wedding ring. Tears were flowing like the Bethesda Fountain as Rev. Van Dyke continued.

> "The ceremony is filled with splendor today. The golden wedding ring belongs to Malachi. It represents his only worldly possession, for it belonged to his beloved mother who died just one year ago. It also represents his love for his new mama and papa who have pledged through adoption to take care of this immigrant son of Ireland

for the rest of their lives. Repeat after me, Lee, 'With this ring, I thee wed'..."

The ceremony ended with the last *Amen* and Lee kissed his bride. The three of them, Lee, Charlotte, and Malachi stood with their arms around each other while the Payne men raised their bows and began to play a beautiful refrain, slow and deliberate at first, and then it got louder and faster, faster still, until the sweetest of all southern songs filled the air in the woods across The Lake and through the whole of The Central Park, for it was *Dixie* in its rarest form, and there was clapping and crying and dancing and the ending of the grandest wedding ceremony that had ever been performed in The Central Park or anywhere else.

Lee looked around at the crowd of people, needing a visual to reflect upon in days to come. One of the newspaper reporters was taking photographs. *There will be memories, he thought.* Even Cavanaugh and Hannigan were clapping and smiling.

Margaret leaned against Jonathan who took her arm and helped her to the carriage.

"I'm sorry, Jonathan, but I have become weary."

"That's understandable, Miss Margaret. I do the same thing sometimes. We'll get you comfortable with some blankets and you can watch all this from the carriage."

"Thank you, son. You're a southern gentleman, indeed. Seeing all of you together makes me feel just fine about leaving Charlotte here with Lee. In fact, it helps me to know that I have done the right thing by making no objection."

"You can be sure Lee is going to treat her like a princess," said Jonathan. "You won't need to worry, Miss Margaret."

The day ended, its grandeur now a memory that would never fade. Lee and Charlotte said their goodbyes and went to their new apartment. Malachi stayed with the Mississippi Boys at the Brownstone and Margaret retired to Gilsey House for rest, while all the other guests went their separate ways.

"I can stay with you, Margaret, if you would like," said Rachel, sensing that Margaret was very tired.

"Oh, no, I will be fine, Rachel. Thank you for everything."

"What are your plans, Margaret?"

"I will hope to spend a little time with Charlotte tomorrow, and the following day, I'll be returning to Lexington on the train."

"We'll make certain that is all taken care of," said Rachel, escorting her to the third floor room at Gilsey House while Dan waited in the carriage. "I'll arrange for room service in the morning, so you can enjoy the lovely corner room and the nice view of Broadway while you have a fine breakfast. I'll never forget the first time I stayed here and did the same thing. It is one of my fondest memories of Manhattan Island."

"I will sleep well thinking about it," said Margaret, "and all the wonderful things that have happened in these few days."

"If you need anything, just call for Maria, your chambermaid. We know her well, and she knows how to get in touch with Mr. Alexander."

"Thank you, Rachel. You and all the Paynes have been more than kind to me."

"Sleep well, dear one," said Rachel, "We will see you tomorrow, maybe around mid-day."

Chapter 24

'Tis High Knowledge—

Lee was troubled that Margaret Elliott would be traveling back to Lexington alone. The more he thought about it, the more he determined he was not going to let that happen. If he were this ill at ease, how must Charlotte be feeling? How could he have just two days ago vowed that he would never allow her to become anxious over anything that he could control? He would make some plans before saying anything to her.

"Charlotte, I know your mother wants to spend time with you today, so I'm going to get us downtown to Gilsey House and leave you there for a few hours. We can hail a carriage and I'll take it back to the Brownstone and make sure Malachi is alright and spend a little time with my family. They will all be leaving tomorrow, too. I'll come back and get you when the sun goes down so you can join us. How does that sound?"

"Perfect! I wondered how this was going to unfold, but as always, Lee, you have the plan. Thank you for thinking of Mama."

"It's easy to think of her and to love her, Charlotte. No wonder you are who you are—for you're the image of her."

He kissed her and made the coffee, then his famous scrambled eggs and crusty bread toast in the oven.

"I hope you're going to do this until we're old and feeble."

"That will be an easy one," he said.

At noon, Lee ran the steps at the Brownstone. Malachi, who had been standing in the window when Lee arrived, met him on the landing of the third floor.

"Papa! I've missed y'."

"I've missed you, too, son."

"But I'm having a splendid time with m' relatives. I think they all love m', and I know I love them. I've learned all about y' Papa, including the episode in Hell Gate."

Lee shivered. "It's a wonder I will even go near the New York Harbor or the Harlem River, or the East River. That was a scary day in my life story."

"I can imagine," said Malachi. "I've heard tales of Hell Gate since I was able to think and talk. But now I will have a real story to tell about my papa, hoping people will believe m'."

"Who told the Hell Gate episode? Jonathan?"

"No. He tried to, but he couldn't get past the thought that y' wer' gone forever, sucked into the depths of the murky black waters of the East River. Papa, I believe like y'r brothers that God saved y'r life by getting y' stuck in that handy grip on the boat. 'Twas like a vice, eh? And He saved y'r life so that y' could save mine."

"Oh, my goodness, Malachi! What a grand example of physical and spiritual salvation! Do you think you may preach one day?"

"Well, here's m' scripture for that sermon—'Greater love hath no man than this, that a man lay down his life for his friends' (John 15:13)."

"Now, I'm convinced, and Malachi, you have the favored dialect of the English language for it—that of an Irishman! And you even gave the location of the verse."

"M' teachers have taught m' that if I'm going to quote from the Bible, I must give the location thereof."

They stood on the landing laughing together, enjoying the company of father and son when Lee told Malachi his plan.

Malachi picked up the brown leather book bag Lee had given him when they first visited Mr. Stewart's store. He loved the smell of it. 'Twas a rich feeling, owning a leather bag. He filled it with a few changes of clothing and other essentials to escort his new grandmother back to Lexington. His first train ride. He could not explain his excitement. Papa had made preparations with Mr. Hannigan and his tutors at McBurney's, and he would only be gone a week, and most of that time would be the train ride.

Lee had said, "Malachi, I need to beg you to do something for me."

"Anything, Papa … y' know I will do anything to help y'."

"Grandmother Margaret will be taking the train back to Virginia tomorrow. I know this is short notice, but I would like for you to go with her, escort her on the ride and stay two nights over then return to the City. I will make all the ticket purchases for you. It's a long ride and there will be several stops there and back to New York. You must listen carefully for your transfers and layovers, but there will be porters to help you. And you must carefully guard your tickets. I know you will be fine. Can you do it? Not to make the decision harder, but it might well be a test of your courage."

"Oh, yes, Papa!" There had been no resistance in his voice, though he had never ridden the train. He wondered why Lee had wanted him to go with Grandmother Margaret. He would ask no questions.

"We have to move quickly. In case of an emergency, you can reach us at the newspaper. Here's what you do," said Lee, handing Malachi a piece of white paper. "Put this in the flap of your book bag and when you get on the train, read it carefully and don't lose this. On this paper is also a list of things you will need to do upon arrival in Lexington, first thing, being to make Grandmother Margaret comfortable in her bed, and call on Dr. Benjamin Walker. His address is on the paper, and he lives just two streets away from Grandmother. Tell her everything you are doing and have her know she must stay in bed until you return. Tell her your Papa instructed you to let Dr. Walker know she has returned from New York. When you see the doctor, ask him to please come to her house and examine her to make sure she is okay. The trip to New York has already taken a toll on her, and by the time she returns to Lexington, well, we will have to see. I have no concern that you will be able to do all of this, son."

"Yes, Papa. I will do my best."

'Twas a sad day as are all farewells. The Sarepta connection left early of a morning on the fifth day of January, 1888, just two days after the beautiful Bow Bridge wedding in The Central Park. A bit of gloom hung over them all, for on the same afternoon, Margaret Elliott and her grandson, Malachi, boarded the Pullman destined for Lexington, Virginia. If it had not worked out that way, that is, for Malachi to accompany her mother on the train, Charlotte may well have had a conniption herself. But as it was, she held her mother in her arms for ever so long, kissing her cheeks and whispering in her ears, "I love you, Mama. I'll love you forever. And Mama, please don't try to go to heaven without me. When you get home, tell Malachi exactly what you need. He loves you, dear Mama. He loves you so much and so do I."

Charlotte released her mother and Malachi took her by the hand. They walked toward the Pullman; he shifted her hand into his right hand and put his arm around her waist. With no trouble at all, he helped her up the steps and into the car. She turned toward Charlotte and feebly waved to her for the last time. The little crowd consisting of Malachi's Mama and Papa, his Great-grandmother Rachel, Mr. Oscar, and Dan waved goodbye until the train was out of sight.

"Can we do this, Grandmother Margaret?" said Malachi.

"I think we just about did, Malachi."

Three days following, weary of the long ride and entertaining the thought of leaving behind the dearest on earth, Margaret Elliott sighed and opened her eyes. She had napped before the last call which would be Lexington. Malachi had been nothing short of an amazing gift from God. She had wanted for nothing, but soon he would be gone and then life would consist of something to which she was not accustomed—aloneness. She had never been one to worry o'er the future, nor had she fretted about something that might or might not take place. Her faith level had been increasingly rising the longer she lived. But a twinge of sadness affected her as she realized Malachi, too, would soon be gone.

"Malachi?"

"Yes, Grandmother."

"May I share something with you?"

"Please, Grandmother."

"This is a good story, though it starts out pretty dark and dismal. You know, all the pleasures of this earth will come to an end. For we do have an end on this earth. We all die. Charlotte doesn't like for me to talk about death. I can understand that, but I'm older and I know more." Margaret cleared her throat and chuckled. Malachi smiled.

"Yes ma'am, Grandmother. You know a lot more."

"Yes, we will all die, but Malachi, may that motivate us to live well." Margaret paused a moment to let the thought sink in and then continued. "Because after this, there awaits a glorious Resurrection. So enjoy our Creator God and the life He has given here, looking forward—"

Malachi looked at the lovely face of Grandmother Margaret. Her voice was angelic. She knew when to lower it and when to be heard without mistake. The smile never left her lips, and her emphasis was always on the right words.

"Malachi, when Charlotte's Papa died, it seemed all the pleasures of this earth just came to an end. But I found out that was not the truth. I finally understood … for Papa, God removed the sting of death long before he died. That was joy in itself. He felt no sting that day on the Chancellorsville Battlefield. I knew him. I knew his faith in God, his love for Jesus, his love for Virginia, and Stonewall Jackson. Every time

Stonewall held up his hand to stay the horses and men behind him, and crossed over on the other side of the river to pray, Charlotte's Papa dismounted and took off his tattered hat to reverence the man of God who was praying for the safety of his men and for all the other soldiers in the Army of Northern Virginia. Papa prayed right along with him. You see, I heard him pray at home in the years before he went to war. I know how he prayed to touch the heart of God, and I know the minute he took that shot to the chest, the sting of death just went right past him."

Malachi didn't care that Grandmother saw him crying. He was touched by her life story.

"Malachi, you know if we live as though we are dying, we really kind of cheat death. That doesn't mean we stop suffering physically. I have suffered for many years. When I tried to figure that out, I failed, knowing that it was not my business, but God's. But I do have thoughts about it. Someone once said when we suffer, God has us hemmed in. I didn't like that at first, but you know we are wandering, unfocused sheep who graze mighty close to the edge of the cliff sometimes. The longer you live, the easier it will be for you to see. Psalm 139 is the chapter for that. God knows our down sitting and our uprising, He understands our thoughts, the path we take, everything. He said there's not a word in my tongue that He does not know. He's been behind me, He's gone before me, and He has had His hand upon me. The Psalmist said … 'that's high knowledge'. No matter where I go, He's there and His hand will guide me and His right hand will hold on to me. He keeps the Light on for me. He even covered me in my mother's womb before I was born. All of this is reason to praise Him for His marvelous works."

Margaret stopped short. She could talk no more and Malachi sensed that she was speaking her own eulogy, only a tribute to Jesus, not herself. He had never heard anything like it.

"Grandmother, 'tis like y' have poured y'r blessing upon m', for y' have taught m' more in one hour than I have learned in all m' life. Papa has done an amazing job, but I will tell him exactly how y' have blessed me, at least with as much as is in m' of remembrance. I do wish I had it written on paper. However, I will enjoy and be blessed by Psalm 139 for the rest of m' life. I will always remember that what y' have given m' is 'high knowledge'. Y've painted m' life with the colors of y'r own, and I thank y' for it."

Carriages lined the trail adjacent to the railroad track, awaiting those who had reached journey's end in Lexington, Virginia. Malachi could see them from the window and hoped he could get one for Grandmother Margaret. She had reached the end of the way herself. He gathered their belongings and sat back down with Margaret until the train came to a stop. It was going to take someone equally as smart as he to juggle everything and manage to hold onto his grandmother at the same time.

"Malachi, I'm sorry you got the hard job of taking care of me."

"This trip has been worth it all, Grandmother. I wouldn't take anything for being with you."

They managed somehow and arrived by carriage at the Elliott home, just three roads past the train station. The carriage driver willingly helped get the baggage to the front porch. For the first time in his life, Malachi beheld a cottage, a small one-story dwelling set back off the tree-lined street and surrounded by a white picket fence. The hardwood trees were bare of leaves, simply awaiting springtime when they would come forth in glorious fashion and once again hover over this little piece of Americana. The two walked the path to the steps. Malachi laid their baggage down and all but carried Grandmother Margaret to the front door, for she was barely able to put one foot in front of the other. Her strength was gone.

"Before you leave Lexington, Malachi, I hope … I hope you can take a few minutes to see … Stonewall Jackson's home and … and the Memorial Cemetery where he and close to three hundred … Confederate soldiers are buried … including Charlotte's papa."

Margaret was struggling to speak. They paused a moment so she could catch her breath.

"Gen. Lee is buried beneath the Lee Chapel at Washington College, which is where he became president at the close of the war. Your papa would be proud that you visited his hero's memorial, and Charlotte would want you to know all about Stonewall's home. We knew them both personally, as did all of Lexington."

"I would love to if you can point me in the right direction tomorrow. Papa has told me all about both of the great generals. I feel like they are part of our family."

Malachi turned down the linens while Grandmother Margaret freshened up and put on her gown and robe. He noticed that she was almost bent double and scarcely could she move. He helped her into bed, assured her he would return quickly, and closed her door. He took the note from his book bag and read it again. Carefully. Dr. Walker first. He opened Margaret's door and found that her eyes were already closed, her breathing shallow. He laid a low burning fire and left.

"Dr. Walker, I'm Margaret Elliot's grandson, Malachi O'Malley Payne."

"She's told me all about you, Malachi, and it's quite a story."

"Yes sir. Y' see, I escorted her home, and m' papa says I'm to come see y' first and let y' know we have arrived. I have to tell y', she is very sick, Grandmother Margaret, and I was wondering if y' would go to her house and check on her. I helped her to bed and told her I was coming to see y'. She was asleep before I could leave the house. I have to go to the market for milk and bread as there is not much in the house, then I will return. I will do that now and go back to the house. Can y' come this afternoon or later today, sir?"

"Of course, Malachi, I'll be there by the time you get back."

'Twas a small town, though the seat of edification in its corner of the world, what with Washington College and Virginia Military Institute being the centers of learning. Malachi had never known anything but the big City, the dirty streets of Lower Manhattan. The melting pot of America was his home and he loved it, especially now that Lee Payne had taken him out of poverty and into hope for a better life. But this little village was full of history, too. Southern history and tomorrow Lee would take some last moments and fill his head and heart with as much of the South as he could. His heritage had expanded to include Miss Margaret. He loved her from the moment he met her just a few days ago. He feared she lay dying even as he walked the hard-packed dirt streets of Lexington, Virginia. He did not want to think about how Charlotte would take the news, for one day soon she would get the word. *Margaret has taken leave of her old body of clay and has gone to her 'house not made with hands eternal in the heavens'.*

Malachi got the milk, some crusty white bread and some potatoes. He would attempt to make potato soup for Grandmother Margaret. She needed food, he was sure. He hurried, suddenly compelled to get back. There was a carriage on the street. It would be the doctor. He raced up the white-washed wood steps and into the cottage.

"How is she, Dr. Walker?"

He motioned for Malachi to follow him into the sitting room.

"Frankly, Malachi, it doesn't look good. Margaret is tired, her heart, so weak I can scarcely hear it. Did she eat anything on the train?"

"Yes, sir, but not much. Just some porridge of sorts. I was going to make her some potato soup."

"That sounds just right, Malachi. Please make sure she eats and give her lots of water. Can you make her a pot of tea?"

"Yes, sir. I'll do that now."

"She can't seem to keep her eyes open. Maybe the tea will help. I'm going to sit by her for awhile and watch her while you make the soup and her tea. Then, Malachi, I think we have to come up with a plan of how to take care of your Grandmother. You need to know, I don't have a lot of hope that she will get much better."

"Yes, sir, Dr. Walker. I will be giving it some thought, m'self."

"Have you read much from Ecclesiastes, Malachi?"

"Yes sir, I've read the entire book. It's the preacher speaking, right? King Solomon himself, probably?"

"Yes, that's exactly right," said the doctor. "He describes life in the light of human suffering and the importance of God in a person's life. You see, life is transitory. We're born, we live, we love, we work, we suffer, we experience a measure of joy—then we leave it all and we die. Without God and His Son, life is empty and meaningless, an enigma. If we dedicate our lives to worldly gain, then we've lost everything."

"Grandmother and I were discussing this very thing on the train. She told me things that I hope to carry to m' own grave. She has touched m' life like no other and I am rich because of it."

"She is an example of the way we need to live," said Dr. Walker. "If she were to awake and talk to me right now, she would be telling me how good God is and how ready she is to see Him."

Malachi retreated to the little kitchen and laid a fire in the cook stove. He searched for the biggest pot he could find, and using common sense, he washed and peeled the potatoes, cut them in small cubes, and hoped he would find some seasoning in Grandmother's cupboard. Salt, pepper and some dried parsley. He added milk and stirred it all together. As he hoped, it was not long before the soup began to thicken slightly from the starchy potatoes. He shifted the wood pieces in the stove to lower the heat and let it cook until the potatoes were soft. He tasted and it was good. *A miracle in itself, he thought.*

Their conversation was now in low tones so that Margaret could not hear. Besides at this point they knew she did not care.

"Dr. Walker, I've been thinking whilst I was in the kitchen. There's really no reason why I can't stay with Grandmother for a few days. We can telegraph Papa and Miss Charlotte and let them know how ill she is and see what they want to do."

"That's a splendid idea, Malachi. And I know a sweet little old Negro woman who dearly loves your grandmother. I'll see if she wants to consider staying with her when you return to New York. I don't know what this is going to do to Charlotte. I wouldn't be surprised if she didn't rush right back here and stay with her mother. That would probably devastate your papa."

"Yes sir, it would. We must pray for the wisdom of Solomon, Dr. Walker."

"You're wise beyond your years, Malachi."

"I took care of m' mother when she was so sick she couldn't lift her head, couldn't eat or anything. She was very young, much too young to die. So I've had that little bit of experience. It hurts a lot to lose someone y' love."

"Malachi, is that you? Who is with you, son?"

"It's Dr. Walker, Grandmother. How do y' feel?"

"I just feel tired, that's all."

"I made y' some potato soup. Can y' take a few sips?"

"I can try."

Dr. Walker put an extra pillow under Margaret's head and talked to her while Malachi went to the kitchen.

"What are you doing here, Ben?"

"Taking care of you, Margaret. Just like I've always done."

"You're a dear friend."

"Yes, and your Malachi is a dear grandson. We've had a good talk while you were taking a nap."

"He amazes me," she said, again closing her eyes.

The dear family doctor tried to coax her into keeping her eyes open, hoping his voice and the smell of food would entice her, but to no avail. He kept talking while, from the kitchen, Malachi prepared a tray with a small bowl of potato soup, a crust of bread, and a cup of tea. Malachi returned, set the tray beside her and commenced to try and feed her. Without opening her eyes, she took a spoon of soup and turned her face toward the wall and refused another. Malachi tried, though he didn't want to force her. He knew what it was like to be half starving and try to eat on a very empty stomach. Once it had made him throw up his insides, actually just last year, for he was a boy from the depths of poverty, and his stomach was empty most of the time.

"I'm sorry," she whispered.

"Yes ma'am, Grandmother. You just take what you can, but you really need to eat a bit more."

"I just need to rest now, son."

"Malachi, I'm going to leave you for the time being. I will bring old Miss Mollie to help you. She's about eighty herself, but spry as a fifty-year old. She will know what to do for Margaret, and if you need me during the night, just run and fetch me. I live right next door to the clinic where you came to see me today. Can you do that?"

"Yes sir, Dr. Walker. Thank y' for coming and staying with us."

"I think you know where we are here, Malachi. You've been down this road before."

"Yes sir." Tears formed in Malachi's eyes as he said good-bye, knowing what was facing him. He pulled the quilt to Grandmother's chin and stoked the fire. He cleaned the kitchen and poured himself a bowl of potato soup. He loathed the thought of eating when he knew Grandmother could not. He also knew he had to maintain his own strength to take care of her.

A tap on the door and Malachi opened it to find Miss Mollie, a wide smile displaying two fine rows of white teeth. He was happy to have company through the night. She hung her coat and scarf on the rack and made herself at home. She was a tiny woman, delightful, and she had known the Elliotts all her life. During the war years, she had spent many a night with Margaret and Charlotte.

The sun had long since dropped in the cold January sky. The moon against the snow gave a nice light, and Malachi lit the lanterns and some candles knowing this could be a long night. He fixed a tray for Miss Mollie, hoping she would eat.

"My goodness, dis be good soup, Malachi. Where did you learn to cook like dis?"

"Actually 'tis the first time I ever cooked potato soup, Miss Mollie. I'm glad y' like it."

"Did Miss Margaret eat some?"

"Just a few bites. Can y' see if she will wake up for y' and try to eat some more. I left it to warm on the stove."

"Where you be from, Malachi?"

"I was born in Ireland, but I came to New York City with m' mother when I was but two years old. I kept m' Irish accent because of m' mother. She died just last Christmas of pneumonia. I was left an orphan until a wonderful southern gentleman adopted me. Miss Charlotte just married that man, m' papa. Now she is m' mother. Does that make sense, Miss Mollie?"

"It sho do. And I'm so glad to meet you, son. It sounds like you are blessed of de Lawd."

"Yes ma'am, Miss Mollie."

"You bring a little bowl of soup and I'll try to get Miss Margaret to eat."

To no avail, Miss Mollie tried. Margaret would not eat. She never opened her eyes, and she didn't speak a word.

"Dr. Walker done tol' me he don' spec yo' Grandmother to make it through the night, Malachi. I think we better pray."

Together the two knelt beside Grandmother's bed and prayed. Mollie pulled the rocking chair close, and Malachi climbed onto Grandmother's bed beside her. She was barely breathing.

"Miss Mollie, I'm sure glad y' came to be with us. I'm feeling pretty lonely right now. 'Tis the first time I've ever been out of New York City, and 'tis all new to me. I've only known m' grandmother for a few days, and y've known her all y'r life."

Mollie began to tell the story of Lexington during the war years, how that Captain Elliott had died with Stonewall and so many other men from his brigade. She told the account of the great Gen. Robert E. Lee as he slowly trotted his horse, Traveller, through town when he came home.

"De senseless Wah was ovah, thank God, but not until so many of our men and boys were dead and gone. Captain Elliott, he be buried in de Stonewall Jackson Cemetery. Miss Margaret, she gon' go to her early grave over grieving for him. She ain't really old enough to be dyin'. Dis town be full of sorrow over all de killin' and hateful actions of de Nawth against de South. Yes, I be black. My ma and pa sailed de ocean in de belly of a ship, chained together, but day survive it all. Day be much bettah off when day got to dis country. Some good people bought dem and set dem free. Ain't dat what Jesus did for us, Malachi?"

"Yes, Miss Mollie." Malachi smiled at the thought, which he had never before entertained.

"We be on de slave block of sin, and Jesus He done paid de price to set us free."

Slavery from the proper viewpoint, he thought. Miss Mollie knows for sure.

"Miss Mollie, y've taught m' many things tonight, but this I will carry with m' forever. I am learning every day of m' life and I will never forget y' for this."

"We be in dis together tonight, Malachi. De Lawd will see us through it."

"Malachi, who's with you, son?"

"Jesus and Miss Mollie, Grandmother."

"Can you hold me, son?"

"Yes ma'am, Grandmother."

Malachi moved to the corner of her bed and lifted his grandmother into his arms. Mollie stood with her head bowed.

"I feel the presence of Jesus, Malachi."

"Yes ma'am Grandmother. He's right here with us."

"I love you, Malachi, and Charlotte, and Lee Payne, and Mollie. I love all my people."

She spoke slowly, but deliberately and sincerely. "Now I see Him, Malachi. You can let go, now. He's got my hand."

Malachi did not let go, but an amazing presence entered her room as she took her last breath. With tears dropping from his cheeks, he held fast to his grandmother. Mollie laid her hand on his shoulder and he felt the love of another child of God. He knew for the second time in his young life that death is not for the faint of heart. But God had sustained. He had given peace, and best of all—he had sent Miss Mollie to help see him through the night. He laid Grandmother back on her pillow and asked Miss Mollie to cover her. He ran from the house, down the white wood steps and across the snow-covered lawn of the sweet Virginia cottage, crying, looking upward into the star-filled sky, thanking God for the sacred privilege of being there for her. *The closest to Heaven y' can get, he thought, is holding someone in y'r arms until they are in the presence of God.* He ran hard toward the clinic and Dr. Walker's home—wishing for his papa.

Chapter

For All of Manhattan—

New York City Winter of 1893

The stark white French doors opened to the balcony, revealing the last remnants of a beautiful winter day on Manhattan Island. Soon the sun would drop behind the buildings as it always did, leaving a bit of gloom, and the fog would move in across the Hudson River. New Yorkers had to quickly seek out a place to watch the slightest sunset.

"There you are," she said, closing the doors behind her to keep the warmth inside the apartment. "I knew I would find you out here."

Charlotte Payne cautiously moved to the balcony rail where Lee was standing, and pulling her shawl tight across her shoulders, she touched his hand then took a step back. She loved the multi-storied building but was still reluctant to give way to the height.

Lee thoughtfully moved to where she stood, drew her near and kissed her.

"Look!" he said, "A few flakes are falling. Are you warm enough?"

"Yes. With you. I love this. Snow reminds me of home."

"Me, too," he said, "though, I'm sure you get much more snow in Virginia than we do in the real South."

Charlotte gave him a tap on the back and said, "How much more of the South could you possibly want than Virginia! We *are* the South! Think Robert E. Lee and Stonewall Jackson!"

Lee laughed at his beautiful wife. "You're absolutely right. Though we had some fire-eating Mississippi generals."

"Indeed. I'll have to give you that. And I'll bet you know all of them."

"I tried my best to memorize them all, their rank and service record. After a while, it all runs together, though, I hate to admit. And I am removed a few years from West Point."

"Lee, you get so close to the rail. And I cannot for the life of me understand how you can stand to do that, much less step out onto those planks that are suspended between heaven and earth without shivering and—and falling—to your death. I get sick just thinking about what could happen to you."

"Well, you can rest a few months, because I'll not be plank-walking in the snow and ice. That I can assure you."

"It will be comforting to know that you'll be ensconced upon your high seat in the office drawing plans for the interior of those fine buildings."

"I do love that. But you must admit, I am a really good plank walker when the weather is in my favor."

Lee pondered a question for a moment and decided to ask it. He could easily be distracted by the sights and sounds of the street below. The fourteen-floor building was on the trolley line, the rails clacking, iron screeching upon iron as it came to an abrupt stop letting folks off, letting folks on, the bell ringing constantly, and the horse hoofs clicking. The carriages moved back and forth across the trolley line hoping to avoid the next one coming up. It was just another hourly phenomenon of New York City, *necessity*, once again, *the mother of invention*, though Plato likely had not realized the depth of this pithy saying in the eons before Christ, that is if Plato truly was the author. At any rate, it could not have been more appropriate.

"Do you miss the Old South, Charlotte?"

"As much as I love this beautiful City—yes! I miss everything about it. Do you, Lee?"

"I think if Grandmother and Oscar had not been here at least part of each of these years, it would have been a lot harder. Do you?"

"Oh, yes. Rachel has been my stronghold through these past few years. Without her I would not know you, Lee."

"What does that mean?"

"I would not know your dreams and passions from a boy."

"My grandmother is an amazing woman and even in her twilight years, she is beautiful and grace-filled. Through the years she blazed a trail for women from both countries—North and South. Let's go inside. You're shivering. But wait—"

He held her close and kissed her again so that all of Manhattan could see.

"I'm waiting for the applause and cheers and the ring of the trolley bell," she said.

"It's a long way to the street, but I think they got the message. At least I hope so. I want the entire City to know how much I love you, Charlotte Payne!"

And as though she were thinking aloud, Charlotte blurted it out—"Do you think we could spend Christmas in the *South* this year?"

"What do you have in mind?" Lee loved that his wife was subtle, unassuming, and spontaneous all at the same time.

"Sarepta," she said. "I've never once been there. You've been to Lexington with me, but we've never taken Christmas in Sarepta, and since Mama died, there is not much reason to go to Lexington every year. Lee, I would love to see Memphis and Holly Springs, and Oxford. And Shiloh—oh, I want to see Shiloh. And, of course, all of your family."

"And I want you to do all of that, Charlotte."

"Can we at least consider it? I want to know all of your old friends there. You've told me so many grand stories."

"Look, Charlotte! Lights flickering on as far as the eye can see. Don't you love the admixture of gaslights and electric?"

"This country girl is still in awe of the lights of the City, Lee."

He touched her face, his angel, he thought, tucking her hair behind the ruby red ribbon.

"That won't do much good when the cold wind gets into it," she said, pulling her long brown hair up and tying it with itself.

"It always amazes me how you do that and so beautifully. Reminds me of the blustery day we walked the bridge for the first time in the month of May, 1883. The wind off the River blew fiercely, announcing that it would be that way in all seasons. And your lovely hair responded just like now."

She brushed the snow from his face and touched his lips.

"You're a fine-looking man, Lee Payne."

"I know, Charlotte!"

"And arrogant," she said.

They laughed and spun around, caught up in the moment.

Lee knew he could not leave Charlotte without an answer. The war had been over for a lot of years, but to a family that had been brutally affected, it was yesterday. They would always remember the drums and fife in the distance. The whispers of the old men sitting on the benches at the square in Sarepta, their heads together so the young ones could not hear their talk of war. The Mississippi Boys led by Captain T.G. Payne, meeting at the cotton gin, over and over again, contemplating the war and making their plans to drop everything and go. And the Lexington Men, gathering at the old Wade's Gristmill in the Shenandoah Valley, a safe place where corn and grains had been ground since 1750. And then one day, they were gone, some of them returned nevermore, including Charlotte's beloved papa. The Battle of Chancellorsville, the hills and valleys of Gettysburg as they lay dying, blood rolling downward into the railroad cut, pooling on the Wheatfield and in the peach orchard, and never stopping until the last call to charge the enemy who, thanks to Mr. Lincoln, increased in size to the point of a massacre and there was no longer hope for winning so the South could be free again. But—there was a binding of the last remnant of a southern people who so loved their country they were willing to fight until Gen. Lee cried, "No more!"

Lee Payne looked up, aware that he had faded into the gray mist of the evening, to a place where he often drifted, to think of his father, Albert Henry, and the brutal death he suffered in the Peach Orchard that hot July day.

Charlotte was still in his arms, having tightened her grip on him for the several minutes he had slipped from her presence, if in mind only. She wiped the beads of sweat from his forehead with her scarf as she had done many times before.

"Sorry!" he said.

"Don't be, Lee."

"Well, I don't know what I would do without you. You're so strong, and your father gave his last full measure just as mine did. And your mother died of a broken heart long before her time."

"I'm right here with you in all of those thoughts, Lee. I'm sorry if it was the mention of Sarepta. I know it takes you back to it all. But, Lee, we have a grand heritage. We must think of ways to prolong it as long as we possibly can. We were stripped of so much. But just think about the beautiful battle flag Joab was able to find in the snow at Gettysburg, a notable story, and it hangs in Yankee Town up on Fifth Avenue—proudly as a symbol of faithfulness to our Country which we will never forget. *They* cannot take that away from us."

"Yes," he whispered, visualizing Joab combing the railroad cut, the Wheatfield, the Peach Orchard, and along the fence on Chambersburg Pike until he uncovered the corner of the *Southern Cross* Rachel had sewn for her boys before they left Sarepta. Jonathan had draped the flag over his father and Albert Henry and buried them in a shallow grave on the field. Lee's Grandmother Rachel had told him everything she knew about the war and its impact on the South. It was like he had been there. Lee thought of his stepfather, Jonathan, taking care of his responsibilities those three days at Gettysburg, then watching, while throwing up his insides, as the Yankees scraped the Confederate dead from the battlefield and buried them in trenches, the flies already swarming the bloody remains. Lee shook with remembrance of the stories.

"I don't want to move," he said." My safest place is in your arms, Charlotte. Can we just stay here a few minutes?"

"Of course, dear heart, as long as you like."

Charlotte knew when to remain silent, and she did. It was true that Lee had not fought in the heinous war, but there were times when they both needed to reflect. After all, both their fathers died a hero's death—one at Chancellorsville, the other at Gettysburg.

He breathed deeply and said, "I'm going to give every consideration to your desires, dear Charlotte. We have but a few weeks to make a decision, determine if this will become possible. Grandmother Rachel and Oscar are there now, which means that likely we can all be together one more time. Maybe we could surprise them."

"Oh, Lee! You're making me so happy, if only for the thought of it. When Cassie and I were waiting in the carriage the day we married, she encouraged me to get to Sarepta as soon as possible just to see your way of life, to swim in McGill Creek, to romp on the soapstone, to swing from the grapevine, to listen to the birds and the chickens and roosters and the cries of the coyotes at night. To ride Lady, Samuel's chestnut mare. And to walk where you walked Lee."

"That was my plan," he said, smiling. "It means we will have to do some Christmas shopping soon, for we dare not make an appearance in Sarepta, Mississippi, without Christmas gifts from New York."

"I'll make a list of all the relatives and the closest of friends," she said. "You will have to check to make sure I've included everyone."

"Yes. And I'll have to get transportation arranged, train tickets and a carriage from Corinth, which is still the closest depot, I believe. Remember small gifts … it must be small gifts, because we'll have to transport them all in a trunk. It's the thought that counts, and we are not as financially blessed as Oscar Alexander, who himself is the most generous soul I know."

"You need to see your family, Lee."

"I don't remember the last year I was there. Do you?"

"No, but you went alone when Isaac's grandchild died. They were all here for your graduation ceremony at West Point. And Jonathan and your mother and the boys came for our wedding."

"It becomes shameful that it's been so long that we can't remember what year it was."

She pulled his face to her shoulder and he said in a muffled voice, "I'm glad you made the suggestion. Now, I will make it happen."

"One more thing we're forgetting."

"What?"

"Malachi must go with us."

"I wasn't forgetting him, and I would never want to go away without him. I just wanted you to be the one who said it."

"Well, I'm glad I did. You will need to let him know soon."

"Yes, today! He will have a conniption."

Epilog

Sweltering Hot Summer—

July, 1894

He tapped Dixie and rode to the Battery, the port of entry and the occupation of New York Harbor by British ships and troops during the Revolutionary War; the hangout for Commander-in-Chief of the Continental Army, Gen. George Washington and his troops; the port of entry and seat of Customs for immigrants from all over Europe—and to Robert E. Lee Payne, so much more. He pulled to the curb and stopped Old Dixie, closed his eyes and reflected on the past. He sat for a moment, relishing the ocean breeze on such a hot day, opened the brown leather journal Grandmother Rachel had given him years ago when he was young. His written words were far from poetic, mostly harsh and colloquial. He read, inhaling memories of the stench of raw garbage in the Bowery and all over the Lower East Side. Just thinking about the hot streets and late summer of 1887 reminded him that *familiarity breeds contempt*, as surely as *Aesop's Fable*, the story of *The*

Fox and the Lion. He was the *Fox* and he had encountered the *Lion* that year. But this was no fable. It was a life story. And re-living it was only momentarily re-casting his pearl before the swine. For after that crucial interval, he had an amazing life in a beautiful part of the City with the woman he loved and with another gift that God gave him out of that loathsome interim when he was like Jonah of old … briefly *in the belly of the whale*.

Lee swallowed hard, wishing for water. He was thirsty, the summer heat and his thoughts consuming him. He wiped the sweat again. He was dredging now—his memory and his journal the devices that would keep him in the past, when he was still single, contemplating marriage to his beloved Charlotte and trying to figure it all out. Malachi O'Malley had miraculously and suddenly come on the scene of Lee's otherwise mundane life and everything had changed. He choked and took short breaths, not desirous of inhaling the noxious odor of remembrance of that despicable night of the insane bare knuckle fighter who clamped down on his shoulder and blood spurted across the filthy mat that covered the boxing ring. He could have died that night, but Malachi would have none of that.

Lee drifted again, still clutching the journal, no longer reading, for the events of the years he had stuffed into his memory, maybe forever, had surfaced one by one as if it were yesterday. He touched his shoulder where some thirty stitches had long-since healed, leaving a deep scar, the only physical remains of a few months of reckless behavior. He took a moment to marvel at God's protection of the young and the foolish, remembering the night Charlotte had seen it for the first time. There was nothing else he could do but clutch the passage of time, and tell her the story. The story of how he really met Malachi O'Malley. He was glad to do it now, because time reconciles all. Funny, but she cried that night and said it was a fine story. It gave them Malachi and what could be better. He had grown to be a man of amazing stature, and in just a few months, he would become a member of the Long Gray Line. Like his father, he had crossed the black waters of the Hudson many times aboard the *Chauncey Vibbard* and he had suffered and endured the trials and tests of brave men whose fathers and grandfathers once went to war and of young men who would, one day, go to war.

Lee knew he was favored to live in the amazing City. But above and beyond his love for the tangible and sophistication of Manhattan, he loved his wife as Gen. John B. Gordon of Georgia had cherished his own. In fact, when Lee read accounts that Gen. Gordon's wife—his *girl wife* as he called her, for she was but a girl when they married—had entrusted their two young sons with her parents and followed Gordon to war—Lee purposed in his heart to endear Charlotte to himself to as great an extent. He had vowed to forever make her happy. She was a remarkable woman, a wife of the same value as Fanny Haralson Gordon, and with a much more beautiful name—Charlotte Jackson Elliott Payne, though Fanny's name was really *Rebecca*.

He read on, recalling his wedding day, The Mississippi Boys playing *Dixie* on their violins, the old Southern song that evoked *the land of cotton and old times never forgotten*. Snow falling on the Bow Bridge in The Central Park. Malachi standing with him so close he could feel the warmth of his presence on that cold and snowy high noon. And just days later, the quick decision to send Malachi to Lexington with Grandmother Margaret, the Irish Immigrant boy's life changing by the minute while he held Charlotte's mother in his arms as she lay dying. It all happened so fast. Malachi was but fifteen years old, an orphan boy raised up on the dirty streets of Lower Manhattan, sleeping on the fire escapes of the tenement dwellings in abject poverty. And then one day, God rescued him, apprehended him, and gave him to Robert E. Lee Payne. From the potato farms of Ireland to the shores of America, the pit of poverty, Lower Manhattan, a tenement dweller at age two, and from a jack to a king by the age of fifteen. Adopted into a household of faith, a *Mephibosheth who would sit at the king's table forever*. A full-fledged Son of the Long Gray Line of West Point Military Academy. Malachi had paid his dues. He considered it a privilege and he would live life to the fullest because he fain would have sat down on a dirty curb on the Lower East Side with a stranger to tell his pitiful story, never dreaming that stranger would one day become his father. Malachi had not seen the sun, but he had seen its distant rays. He had not touched a rainbow, but he had seen its prismatic hues. Everything good that life could offer, the young Irishman had seized and celebrated as a *good and perfect gift* from God, and all of this he considered to be *high knowledge.*

Lee found it hard to believe that his son was now twenty-one years old and graduating from West Point. Malachi's path had been his father's portion, and now he knew the life stories of the great generals, Robert E. Lee and Stonewall Jackson and John B. Gordon, A.P. Hill and Henry Heth. And, like his adoptive forebears, with all his heart and soul, he had given an immigrant's contribution to a country that had loved him and taken him in as one of its own.

Together father and son had inherited courage and the miraculous faith of their fathers.

Jane Bennett Gaddy
2018—

Notes

For more than a century, the number of casualties of the War for Southern Independence has been reported as 620,000. The most recent count was revised to a much higher number of an average of 750,000. Not just combat casualties. Illnesses, suicide, heat strokes, and all other war-related deaths are all included in this number.

If you have read and researched Civil War history, you know that many historians hold a heavy bias toward the North and Lincoln. I fear they failed to read the hearts and letters of the men and boys who fought for the South. When I first learned about the letters my ancestors wrote from the killing fields of the war, I was ecstatic. I could not have written my stories without those letters, which had been re-typed from the originals and back-to-back printed and hard bound. The originals are single filed in separate folders and archived at the University of Mississippi Library. My great-grandfather, Samuel Clark, faithfully relinquished ownership and donated them so that everyone with an interest would be able to see and read them. You could not tell those Mississippians they were fighting for slavery, for they didn't own a single slave. Very few families in Northeast Mississippi did. Little is ever mentioned about slave owners in the North, in the East, in New England. All responsibility was laid at the feet of the South.

My Confederate descendants are Thomas Goode (T.G.) and Marjorie Brown Rogers Clark (Rachel in my stories), Jonathan, Albert Henry, Isaac, Joab, and Samuel, who was but two years old when his father and brothers went to war. T.G., Jonathan, and Albert Henry fought in Lee's Army of Northern Virginia and all three died at the Battle of Gettysburg on July 1 and 3, 1863. As you know by now, after reading the six books in the series, I brought Jonathan home. I couldn't bear to lose both boys in my story. Isaac went to war when he reached age seventeen, which was after the death of his father and brothers. He fought to the end of the war and returned home to Slate Springs.

Oscar Alexander, Robert E. Lee Payne, Charlotte Jackson Elliott, Margaret Elliott, Malachi O'Malley, Hannigan, Cavanaugh, Carlisle and Kathryn Peterson are fictional characters. I created them to take the story to New York City. The war had significant effects on the people, the economy, the newspapers, the railroads; and in Lower Manhattan, the Draft Riots of 1863 affected the morale of the City.

Much is archived that reveals the unsavory activities of Lincoln and his Radical Republican Regime, such as his relationships with Karl Marx, Communist, and Friedrich Engels, Marxist, and other communists who supported Lincoln's Regime and who communicated with him either in person or by means of the northern newspapers.

Civil War Generals, pastors, department store owners, and other local New Yorkers mentioned were real people of the era.

The New York Elite Press is a fictional newspaper. Other newspapers mentioned were real and the events that took place are archived in public domain. Historians would do well to avail themselves of these archived newspapers as they research the war years.

Resources

> The mention of Francis Scott Key (1779-1843) is from his life story, excerpts written by Rick Williams, *Chalcedon Magazine*. Key was a devout Christian with an unsullied testimony. He wrote *The Star Spangled*

Banner while imprisoned on a British battleship as he watched the "bombs bursting in air" at Ft. McHenry in Baltimore.

Very interesting and informative reading at *LibriVox: Acoustical liberation of books in the public domain. Fourteen Months in American Bastiles,* Francis Key Howard (1826-1872); Online Audio Book with introduction by Katie Riley, Genre(s): War & Military, Memoirs, Modern (19th C).

Francis Key Howard, Francis Scott Key's grandson, fifty years later, was in that same Federal prison where the flag blew in the wind that day as his grandfather penned the words to *The Star Spangled Banner.* Howard was imprisoned at the orders of Union General George B. McClellan for writing a critical editorial in the *Baltimore Exchange*, of which Howard was the editor. The charge—opposition to Lincoln's suspension of the *writ of habeas corpus*, and imprisoning, without due process and under martial law, the mayor of Baltimore, Congressman Henry May, the police commissioners of Baltimore, and the entire city council. He said, "As I stood upon the very scene of that conflict, I could not but contrast my position with his, forty-seven years before. The flag which he had then so proudly hailed, I saw waving at the same place over the victims of as vulgar and brutal a despotism as modern times have witnessed."

A fascinating online archived account of Sherman's war activities are his letters to his wife, Ellen, written during the war years (1861-1865). On his March to the Sea, his plan was to annihilate the women and children of the

South. He expressed this to his wife in one of the letters. She wrote back: "Kill them all."

The South Was Right, James Ronald and Walter Donald Kennedy, Pelican Publishing Company, Gretna 2006.

Tithes of Blood, A Confederate Soldier's Story, Billy Ellis, *Journal of Confederate History Series*, Vol. XVIII, John McGlone, Series Editor, Southern Heritage Press, 4035 Emerald Drive, Murfreesboro, TN 37130. The men of this story fought alongside my descendants in Lee's Army of Northern Virginia. This book was given to me by Starke Miller, Oxford, University of Mississippi, and Shiloh Historian.

Lifework and Sermons of John L. Girardeau. The State Company, Columbia, SC, 1916., Chapter IV, Confederate Chaplain, p. 106.

Lee After the War, Marshall W. Fishwick, Dodd, Mead & Company, New York, 1963.

The New York History Blog (Historical News and Views from the Empire State) gives a typical account of the New York City Draft Riots of 1863.

There are many such articles written and some historical fiction books include the account. Interestingly, no monuments or remembrances are erected to the historical event; the Draft Riots remain the most significant insurrection by civilians in American history. Fernando Wood was Mayor of New York City at the time. He opposed the Thirteenth Amendment and voiced his support for the Confederate States during the war, suggesting to the City Council that New York

City secede from the U.S. and declare itself a "free city" in order to continue its profitable cotton trade with the South so that the Democrat machine could maintain the revenues which depended on Southern cotton.

Encyclopedia Britannica Peter Cooper and Cooper Union, American Inventor and Manufacturer, and *ASME—The American Society of Mechanical Engineers:* Peter Cooper Biography.

About the Author

Thou shalt guide me with thy counsel,
and afterward receive me to glory.
Whom have I in heaven but thee?
and there is none upon earth that
I desire beside thee.
(Psalm 73:24-25)

Jane Bennett Gaddy is a true daughter of the South. Born in the Mississippi Delta in 1940, a mere seventy-five years after the close of the War Between the States, she writes with passion about her forebears who fought and died in the heat of battle and the family that was left behind to endure the aftermath. Her stories are fiction for who can know all the little nuances of a life, much less the poignant details that Jane Gaddy showers upon her readers. She holds vigil over the history of the South, the facts irrefutable. And to authenticate the family side of her novels are the letters her great-great grandfather and his sons wrote home while they were at war, the letters back to the fighting men from her great-great grandmother, likely strewn and blood-bespattered across the peach orchard, the wheat field, and the railroad cut of the Gettysburg Battlefield where the Clark men found their final resting place on July 1 and 3, 1863.

Gaddy is the author of ***House Not Made With Hands***, a poignant memoir that first sparked the writing of her historical fiction series that presently consists of six novels—***The Mississippi Boys*** published in 2008; ***Isaac's House***, 2011; ***JOAB***, 2013; ***Rachel, After the Darkness***, 2014, ***To Love Again***, 2016; and ***Inherited Courage***, 2018.

She holds a Ph.D. in Religion; administers a course in American Literature and English Composition for external studies students of Bethany Divinity College and Seminary in Alabama; and she edits manuscripts and assists her clients all the way to the publisher. She is a proud member of the United Daughters of the Confederacy through Captain Thomas Goode (T.G.) Clark, Company F, 42nd Mississippi Infantry Regiment, Joseph Davis Brigade, A.P. Hill Corps, Henry Heth Division, Army of Northern Virginia, General Robert E. Lee, Commander. Her genealogy extends to Lieutenant Jonathan Clark of Christian County, Kentucky, who fought in the Kentucky militia in the Revolutionary War.